JUDGMENT DAY

LEFT BEHIND

>THE KIDS<

Jerry B. Jenkins

Tim LaHaye

WITH CHRIS FABRY

TYNDALE HOUSE PUBLISHERS, INC.
WHEATON, ILLINOIS

Visit Tyndale's exciting Web site at www.tyndale.com

Discover the latest Left Behind news at www.leftbehind.com

Published in association with the literary agency of Alive Communications, Inc., 7680 Goddard Street, Suite 200, Colorado Springs, CO 80920.

Edited by Curtis H. C. Lundgren

ISBN 0-8423-4295-8

Printed in the United States of America

08 07 06 05 04 03 02 01
9 8 7 6 5 4 3 2 1

To Kristina, Christopher, Kristin, and Doug

TABLE OF CONTENTS

What's Gone On Before

JUDD Thompson Jr. and the other kids in the Young Tribulation Force are involved in the drama of a lifetime. The global vanishings have left them alone, and now a worldwide earthquake has killed their friend, Ryan Daley.

Vicki Byrne, sixteen, struggles to deal with Ryan's death. An odd young man, Charlie, helps her bury Ryan near the site of New Hope Village Church. Vicki learns from Chaya Stein's father that Chaya was also killed in the earthquake. Mr. Stein does not want to hear more about Vicki's faith.

With the help of his biker friend, Pete, Judd makes it back to Mount Prospect.

Lionel Washington, suffering from loss of memory, is now a Global Community Morale Monitor and returns to his hometown. When Vicki is accused of murdering her high school principal, Lionel gets involved.

Finally, Lionel's memory is restored, but it's too late for the kids. The leader of the Morale Monitors, Commander Blancka, is on his way.

Follow the Young Trib Force as they try to stay out of the hands of the Global Community and change their world one person at a time.

ONE

The Hiding Place

LIONEL saw the chopper and had to do something. Judd and Vicki looked scared. *They should be,* Lionel thought. *I have to get rid of Melinda and Felicia.*

The two Morale Monitors started toward the chopper, then turned.

"You two go and get Blancka," Lionel said. "We'll let him sort out this mess."

"They could run," Melinda said, nodding toward Judd and Vicki.

"I'm staying," Felicia said.

Lionel grabbed his gun. "If they run, I'll shoot 'em."

The girls hesitated.

"Conrad and I can handle these two," Lionel said. "Go! The commander will be waiting."

Melinda and Felicia ran toward the chopper, and Lionel put away his gun. "We have to hurry. Conrad, I'm assuming you're with us."

"I don't know about this God stuff," Conrad said, "but I'm with you."

"Vick and I need to get out of here," Judd said. "Question is whether you guys go with us."

"We should work behind the scenes for now," Lionel said.

"You're crazy," Conrad said. "I don't want to stay here."

Lionel shook his head.

"It's almost dark," Judd said. "They won't be able to see us soon."

"We could hide or find what's left of my house," Vicki said.

"No way," Conrad said. "The chopper's high-tech. Lights, night vision, even heat sensors. They'll spot you in two minutes."

"Time's running out," Vicki said. "If we stay here, that commander guy—"

Judd cut her off. "Ryan's place. Under the church."

"You think we can get in there?" Vicki said.

"It's worth a shot," Judd said. "Could the chopper find us under all that concrete?"

"Yeah," Conrad said. "It wouldn't be easy, but they'd still spot you."

"Not if they think we ran," Judd said. "You

two cover for us and send them the wrong way."

"If they'll believe us," Conrad said.

Judd took Lionel's flashlight. It was pitch black inside the church basement.

"You sure this is where Ryan's hideout was?" Vicki said.

"We're close," Judd said.

"Look stable?" Lionel said.

"Can't tell," Judd said, pulling at loose stones and dirt.

"Another tremor and you guys will be smashed," Conrad said.

Judd held the light while Vicki climbed through the opening. A block fell near Vicki with a sickening thud and she froze. Gathering herself, she continued.

When she reached the bottom she called out, "There's an old steel desk down here that should protect us."

Judd followed her inside. When he heard chopper blades, he turned. "What about you guys?"

Lionel pushed him. "We're OK."

"No," Judd said. "If those girls find us gone, they'll know you helped." Judd climbed out of the hole.

Lionel looked over his shoulder. "Get back inside!"

Conrad held out his gun to Judd.

"What?"

"Take it and smack me underneath the eye," Conrad said. "I'll tell them you overpowered me."

"I can't hit you."

"You're saving us both," Conrad said.

Judd took the gun and carefully hit Conrad just under his eye.

Conrad frowned. "My grandmother can hit harder than that." But his eyes watered and a red mark rose on his cheek.

"Get in there!" Lionel said, ripping the radio from Conrad's shoulder and tossing it into the hole. "Sit tight and keep an ear on that. We'll be in touch."

Judd climbed into the darkness and followed Vicki's voice to the steel desk.

A shot rang out. Then two more.

"What was that?" Vicki said.

"Lionel," Judd guessed. "Hope he knows what he's doing."

Lionel had keyed his microphone when he fired. He wanted the commander to believe he and Conrad were hot after Judd and Vicki.

But he also wanted to scare Phoenix away. It worked. Phoenix darted into the rubble of the neighborhood and disappeared.

Lionel keyed his mike. "This is Washington! The suspects are getting away! Graham got knocked down!"

Commander Blancka sounded enraged. "What's going on down there?"

"The guy hit him, sir," Lionel said, waving for Conrad to run with him. Lionel was out of breath. "He grabbed Conrad's gun! I got a couple of shots off!"

Lionel heard Melinda protest in the background. Commander Blancka said, "Where are they now?"

"We're in pursuit," Lionel said. "East of the ruined church. Send the chopper!"

Silence.

Come on, Lionel thought, *believe me!*

A few moments later the commander barked, "Washington and Graham, bring it in."

"They're getting away!"

"That's an order!"

Judd squeezed under the desk with Vicki. He turned the radio down. The dust made him cough. It felt good to be close to Vicki again.

There was a long silence. Vicki finally spoke. "I can't believe Ryan's not coming back. Why would God let that happen?"

Judd shook his head. "I remember how hard it was for Ryan when Bruce died. It was hard on all of us, but him especially. Now I know how the little guy felt."

"He hated you calling him that," Vicki said.

Judd nodded. "He had a lot of heart. He never gave up."

Vicki sniffed, and Judd could tell she was wiping her eyes. "Sometimes it feels like God doesn't care," she said. "Like he's a million miles away."

Judd's leg cramped and he scooted lower under the desk. He braced himself on the bottom of the desk drawer and felt paper taped to the underside. Carefully, he loosened a thick packet.

"What is it?" Vicki said.

Judd put the envelope on the floor and cupped his hands around the end of the flashlight. In the dim light Judd saw Ryan's name on the front of the envelope. Judd tore it open and looked inside.

"Verses," Judd said as Vicki held the light. "Bruce's handwriting."

Judd read aloud, "Ryan, if you ever lose hope, this will help you. Isaiah 40:30-31."

> Even youths will become exhausted, and young men will give up. But those who wait on the Lord will find new strength. They will fly high on wings like eagles. They will run and not grow weary. They will walk and not faint.

Judd stuffed the envelope in his pocket. "There's a whole stack of those. And stuff Ryan wrote about talking to people about Christ."

"We'll read it later, right?" Vicki said.

"For sure."

It was dark when Lionel and Conrad reached the commander. Melinda and Felicia stood near him with arms folded.

Before the commander spoke Lionel said, "Start east of the church."

"We'll handle it," the commander said, inspecting Conrad's eye. "How'd you get this?"

"Guy hit me with my own gun," Conrad said. "Made Lionel put his down too."

"Lucky he didn't kill you," the commander said. "Where's your radio, Conrad?"

"Must have lost it in the struggle."

Felicia smirked. "Or maybe you two gave it to them."

Lionel turned on her. "We almost get killed, and you—"

"Enough!" Commander Blancka said. He radioed the chopper pilot. "Search the area. Let us know when you have something."

"I'm telling you, sir," Felicia said, "these two were like big pals with Lionel. Why wouldn't they take his gun?"

"How should I know?" Lionel shot back.

"He's helping them," Felicia said.

"Enough," the commander said.

"Sir, request permission to help in the search," Lionel said.

The commander said, "You're here at base until this gets straightened out."

"But, sir—"

"You're staying. Is that clear?"

The radio squawked. "Got something, sir."

Vicki held her breath as the chopper flew overhead. Judd whispered, "Sorry to get this close, but the smaller we are the better."

"It's OK."

Vicki was glad Judd was back and safe, but their troubles were starting again. She had told God she would do anything to help others come to know him, but she wanted just one day where everyone she loved was safe. Every time she thought of Ryan she felt a pain in her chest.

The chopper hovered, then turned south and away from them.

"What happens if they catch us?" Vicki said.

Judd put his head against the desk and sighed. "Lionel's smart. He'll lead them the other way."

"Then where do we go?" Vicki said. "Every place we know is flattened. The GC are crawling all over the shelters. They're sure to spot us there."

"How about Darrion's house?" Judd said. "That bunker Mr. Stahley built under the hill was like a steel fortress. If the hill hasn't collapsed around it, we might be able to get inside."

"That's pretty far away," Vicki said. "I don't see how we can get there on foot."

"We'll have to find a vehicle," Judd said. "What do you think?"

"I'm willing to give it a shot. We just need to—"

Judd put a finger to Vicki's lips. "Someone's outside."

TWO
The Visitor

JUDD's heart beat furiously. Someone was trying to get in. Dirt and rocks fell.

Judd picked up a stone. He wouldn't be taken prisoner by the GC again. Judd thought about running. If the chopper pinpointed their position, they were easy targets.

Vicki grabbed Judd's arm and whispered, "What if it's Lionel?"

Judd shook his head. "He would have said something."

Judd eased out for a better look. The ghostly moon glowed through the hole. Suddenly, a figure appeared in the entrance. Judd braced himself and tried not to breathe. The figure stepped toward the hideout, then backed away.

A high-pitched whine, then breathing. Judd stood. "Be right back," he said.

"Don't," Vicki said.

But Judd crawled away. He returned and plopped Phoenix down between them.

"Hello, boy!" she said. Phoenix licked Vicki's face.

Judd placed Phoenix on top of the desk and said, "Stay!" Phoenix put his head down and whimpered.

"Maybe they'll see him and not us," Judd said.

"I wish he'd brought us something to eat," Vicki said.

Lionel stayed with Commander Blancka's aide while the others followed the chopper. He and the aide set up a tent for the commander.

A few minutes later the group trudged in. Conrad winked at Lionel. The commander held Vicki's friend Charlie by the shirt and dragged him inside.

When he first met the boy, Lionel thought Charlie was strange. Charlie wouldn't look him in the eye. His hands and feet were always moving.

"I told you I don't know where they are," Charlie said nervously.

"Let's start over," the commander said. "How do you know them?"

"I met the girl at the store, or the hospital, whatever you want to call it," Charlie said. "My sister was killed in the big earthshake. So I went over—"

"Focus!" the commander shouted. "How did you know this guy and girl?"

"I helped the girl," Charlie said, shaking. "We carried the kid over here and buried him one night. Real spooky."

"You buried a body?" the commander said.

"She asked me to help, so I did."

The commander looked to Melinda and Felicia. "Is that the girl accused of murder?"

"Yes, sir," Melinda said. "Sounds like more than one."

Lionel knew Vicki hadn't killed Mrs. Jenness, and to think she had harmed Ryan was crazy. But he couldn't say anything.

Conrad tugged Lionel's sleeve and nodded toward the door. "Back in a few," he whispered. "Cover for me."

Lionel nodded. Conrad slipped into the night as the commander continued with Charlie. "What did you do after you helped them bury the body?"

"I talked with that guy about his head," Charlie said.

"His head?"

"They had a club and I wanted to join. If you made it, they put something on your head that people outside the club couldn't see. If I believed like they do I'd get a thing on my head. Something about God and how all the people disappeared."

Lionel was sweating. Charlie knew Vicki and Judd were his friends. Would he tell the commander? Lionel tried to stay out of Charlie's sight.

"I got kicked out of the store where my sister worked," Charlie continued, "so I came here. They told me to wait, and I did till that big helichopper came. Didn't like all the noise. I ran away."

"And you have no idea where they are now?" the commander said.

"Last I saw they were down by that kid's grave. The girl cried. She gave me this." Charlie held up a Bible. "I think she was real sorry about him dying."

"Sorry for killing him," Melinda said, "or sorry she might get caught."

Lionel fumed.

The commander threw the Bible in the corner. "We'll go to the church." He looked for Conrad.

"He went to get his eye checked, sir," Lionel said.

"Keep an eye on that guy," the commander

told Lionel. "Send Graham our way when he gets back."

Judd told Vicki more about his escape from the GC. "I told the people in the cave my name. I figure they passed it on to the GC."

"But the quake knocked out most of the communication lines," Vicki said.

"They're going up all over," Judd said. "It's like Carpathia was ready for this. The information will get back that I'm not dead. If they catch me now, who knows where they'll send me?"

Phoenix growled and the hair on his back stood straight. "Easy, boy," Judd said. "We need you right where you are."

Someone fell into the room with a thud. Phoenix barked, and Judd and Vicki stared into the beam of a flashlight.

"Good," Conrad said. "I thought you might have run." He brought them up-to-date.

"That Charlie is bad news," Judd said.

"He's sweet," Vicki said. "He deserved to hear the truth."

Judd said, "Conrad, you'd better get back before they miss you."

"Not yet," Conrad said. He sat cross-legged

in front of the desk. "By daylight we might be able to move you."

"You think it'll be safe then?" Judd said.

"Lionel will have a plan." Conrad scooted closer. "I also came down here because I want to know more."

"About what?" Vicki said.

"About God. You know, the forehead stuff."

Phoenix sat up again and bristled.

"Guess we can't talk now," Conrad said. "Later?"

"I don't think we'll be getting much sleep," Judd said.

"If we have to run," Vicki said, "tell Lionel we'll try to make it to the Stahley house. He should tell Darrion and Shelly to meet us there."

"I don't know where that is, but Lionel will, right?" Conrad said.

"Right. Darrion can lead you there if she needs to."

"Sit tight as long as you can," Conrad said as he crawled through the entrance. He looked back at Phoenix. "And keep him quiet."

Lionel sat Charlie down and looked at him sternly. "You know Vicki didn't kill Ryan."

"I know, but the big man talks mean, and I'm scared he's going to yell at me."

"You have to tell the truth."

"You're one of them, aren't you?" Charlie said.

Lionel nodded. "But don't tell the commander, OK?"

"I won't if you tell me how I can get a thing on my head."

Lionel pulled up a chair. "Charlie, this isn't a club. And you can't be part of the group if all you want is something on your head."

"Then how can I join?"

Lionel struggled to remember his own story. His past with the other kids had flooded back quickly. Now, as he talked with Charlie, he relived the moment when he finally understood the truth.

"I treated church like a club when I was a kid," Lionel said. "It was just a place to hang while my parents sang and did their Bible study."

"So you didn't have the thing on your forehead back then?"

"Charlie, stop talking about the mark and start listening."

"Right, got it. Start listening."

"The thing I missed was that God is real.

He made you and me for a purpose. And he wants us to know him."

"I believe that," Charlie said. "I don't think we got evolved or came from monkeys or whatever they say we came from."

"Good," Lionel said. "But it's not enough just to believe God exists. He offers each of us a gift."

"You mean the thing on—"

"Stop with that!" Lionel shouted. Charlie shrank in his chair. "God offers everybody forgiveness. When I first met Judd and Vicki, I didn't even know I needed it. I was so scared because all my family had disappeared. Deep down I knew I'd missed the most important thing. I had never asked Jesus to forgive me. That's the gift. If you ask God to come into your heart and forgive you—"

Commander Blancka's aide returned.

Vicki held Phoenix and tried to keep him quiet. She strained to hear voices outside.

"This is where they were standing," a girl said.

"And this is the grave?" a deep-voiced man said. "Dig it up."

Vicki looked at Judd in horror. Judd put a finger to his lips.

Vicki heard Conrad, out of breath. "Sir, I saw movement near a house about a hundred yards back."

Commander Blancka radioed the pilot the information, and Vicki heard chopper blades.

"Located your radio?" Commander Blancka said.

"Not yet, sir," Conrad said.

"That's easy enough," the commander said. He keyed his microphone. "Commander Blancka requesting a radio locate."

"What's that, sir?" Conrad said.

"The radio has a homing device. Let us find you."

The radio squawked. "Commander Blancka, we need the ID number for the radio."

Vicki quickly turned off the radio. They had to get rid of it.

THREE
Night Meeting

LIONEL heard the commander's call and knew Judd and Vicki still had Conrad's radio.

"Where you going?" the aide said as Lionel stood to leave.

"I'm done baby-sitting. I'm going to catch these two."

"But the commander—"

"When I turn them in, he'll be glad," Lionel said as he rushed through the door of the tent. "Keep an eye on Charlie."

As he ran toward the church, Lionel formed a plan. He would tell the commander he had helped Judd and Vicki escape. They were long gone. The GC would court-martial him or worse, but Lionel didn't care.

Lionel felt guilty. If he had only said no to the man who had taken him south. If he had resisted the GC training after his accident. He shook his head. He couldn't think about that now. He had to get to the commander before anyone found Judd and Vicki.

Lionel's radio squawked. "We've got that locate you wanted on the radio, sir."

"Give me the coordinates," Commander Blancka said.

"Sir, the unit is moving."

"That means they're on the run!" the commander said. "Where are they?"

"From the description of your own location, I'd say they're only a few yards away."

Lionel's heart sank. The underground shelter had become Judd and Vicki's prison. Lionel had given them Conrad's radio. *How could I be so dumb!* he thought.

Lionel swore.

So, he thought, *there's some of that still in me.* He picked up his pace and neared the group. The helicopter was in position over the church with its lights trained on the commander and the others.

"Somebody's running!" Melinda shouted, drawing her gun.

Lionel shouted and held up his hands.

"What are you doing here?" the commander shouted. "I told you—"

"Sir, I have something I need to tell you," Lionel said.

The pilot said, "They're a few yards to your right."

"Sir," Lionel said.

"Hang on to it!" the commander shouted.

"This is important, sir," Lionel said.

"Commander, look!" Conrad shouted, pointing to a figure in the shadows.

Melinda and Felicia pointed their guns toward the figure. Lionel fumbled with his own gun, then turned, hoping he wouldn't see Judd and Vicki with their hands up. He gasped when he saw Phoenix bounce out of the shadows and into the beam of the search-light. Conrad's radio was neatly tied around the dog's neck. Phoenix sat and put his paw in the air.

"It's a dog!" the commander shouted into his radio. "They're not here! Keep looking!"

The chopper flew away. Melinda and Felicia moved toward Phoenix, their guns still up. Phoenix growled. "He might be booby-trapped," Felicia said.

"Booby-trapped, my eye," the commander said. He strode past them and unhooked the radio from the dog's back. "They're taunting us with this dog, trying to make us look like fools. They're probably miles from here at one of the shelters by now. Probably gettin' a good night's sleep while we're out here hunting them down."

"What should we do, sir?" Conrad said.

"We're gonna find 'em," the commander said. "Not one of us is going to stop until we find those two."

Felicia objected when the commander told each of them to go in a different direction. "I don't trust Lionel," she said.

"Fine," the commander said. "He goes with you."

"But—"

"No buts!" the commander barked. "Graham, strap your radio on and follow this dog. See if he leads you anywhere. And Washington, what was it you were going to say a minute ago?"

"It's not important now, sir," Lionel said.

Vicki trembled. "Do you think it worked?"

"The chopper moved away," Judd said. "That's a good sign."

They sat still a few minutes, waiting for someone to burst into their hiding place, but no one came.

They had outfitted Phoenix with the radio and pushed him out the entrance. In the noise and confusion they had gone unnoticed, and Phoenix had done exactly what they wanted. He had gone away from the church.

"What now?" Vicki said.

"We wait," Judd said.

"But they'll see us through the chopper's heat sensor," Vicki said. "I think we ought to bolt while we have the chance."

"That's what they want us to do," Judd said, "lose our cool and run."

Vicki frowned. "I'm not losing my cool; I'm looking for our best options."

"I didn't mean it like that," Judd said. "They think we're on the run. We'll hide here until Lionel tells us to move."

"What if we split up?" Vicki said. "Wouldn't that give us a better chance?"

"Not with that chopper," Judd said. "I think we should stick together and wait to hear from Lionel."

Vicki felt cramped under the desk. "Let me outta here," she said. "My legs are going to sleep."

Vicki shoved her way out and knocked over a pile of rocks.

"Watch it!" Judd said.

"Just because you're a year older doesn't mean you can boss me around," she said. "You're doing the same thing you did with

Ryan! You bossed him and made him feel like a jerk!"

Judd hung his head. "I want to talk, but if you don't whisper, you'll lead them right to us."

"You're doing it again," Vicki whispered. "You don't think I know we need to be quiet?"

"We have a different opinion about our next move," Judd said, "but we're on the same team. We both want to get out of here alive and stay away from the GC."

"We do have that in common," Vicki said.

Judd sighed and turned his head.

"What is it?" Vicki said.

"The truth is, I feel a sense of responsibility for you."

Vicki bristled.

"Not like you're my child," he continued, "but my friend who I wouldn't want anything bad to happen to." Judd's voice cracked. "Vicki, I really care about you. And believe me, I've kicked myself a thousand times for the way I treated Ryan."

"I know you care," Vicki said.

"It's your call," Judd said. "If you want to run, I'll go with you."

"We'll stay," Vicki said as she crawled under the desk. "I'm sorry for saying that about Ryan."

Judd nodded and sat beside her. She put a hand on his shoulder. He seemed so tired.

Judd awoke twenty minutes later as Conrad slipped into their hiding place.

"I could only talk to Lionel for a minute, but he agreed with me," Conrad said. "We'll create a diversion after I leave and get you two out of here. This place is going to be crawling with GC by morning."

"Are we that important?" Vicki said.

"The commander's taking it personally. He wants you two bad."

Conrad went over the plan and made sure their watches were in sync. He also said they would find Shelly and Darrion and get them to the Stahley mansion as soon as possible.

"Something else," Conrad said. "If the GC get close, remember, they have guns. We have orders to shoot to kill."

Judd looked at Vicki.

"And if they catch you, don't do anything stupid. Lionel and I will figure out something."

"What if the Stahley place is destroyed?" Vicki said.

"There's a picnic area in the forest preserve behind it," Judd said. "We can meet there."

The commander's voice blasted over the radio. "Graham, where are you?"

"Still following the dog, sir. No sign of them yet."

"Roger. Keep an eye on him. Out."

Conrad rolled his eyes. "I have a few minutes before we put the plan in motion. Would you mind telling me more about the God thing?"

"How much do you know?" Judd said.

"I've checked out the rabbi a couple of times on the Web. I know all the stuff that's happening was predicted in the Bible."

"It took us a while to figure it out," Judd said. "A pastor who got left behind helped us. He's gone now, but the message is the same."

"Which is what?" Conrad said.

"God came back for his true followers, and a lot of people who thought they were religious didn't make it."

"Why not?"

"Because it's not about being religious," Judd said. "It's about a relationship with God through Jesus Christ."

"What does that mean?" Conrad said.

Vicki jumped in. "I had the same question. My parents changed big-time and wanted me to. They kept saying I should accept Jesus. It wasn't until they disappeared that I figured it out. Accepting him means you admit you can't get to God on your own. You ask him to forgive you for the bad stuff you've done. And with me there was plenty of bad stuff."

"Me too," Conrad said.

While Vicki told more of her story, Judd turned on a flashlight and grabbed a small Bible from Ryan's stash. He showed Conrad verses in Romans that said everyone had sinned.

"I read that on the Web site," Conrad said, "but it didn't make sense until now."

"You can pray anywhere," Judd said. "Even here."

"Yeah," Conrad said. "How do I do it?"

Judd led Conrad in a short prayer. "God, I know I've sinned. I'm sorry. Please forgive me. I believe Jesus died for me and came back from the dead. I accept your forgiveness right now. Come into my life and change me. Amen."

Judd handed Conrad a Bible. "Did you get to talk to my brother about any of this?" Conrad said.

"Ryan and I got to talk about God with him," Judd said. "He heard the truth."

"But he didn't believe, did he?"

Judd turned his head. "He didn't tell me he believed, but only God knows his heart."

Conrad nodded and pointed to Vicki's forehead. "I can see it," he said. "No matter what happens now, at least I know I'll see you guys again."

Lionel glanced at his watch. The plan would go into effect in two minutes. He hoped Conrad had made it to the hiding place.

Felicia and Melinda continued to eye him as they walked through the rubble. They had searched two shelters and were heading to a third when Conrad's call came in.

"This is Graham," Conrad said. Phoenix was barking wildly in the background. "I think I just spotted them. Their dog's goin' crazy over here."

"Location!" Commander Blancka shouted.

Conrad gave his position. Conrad was leading them away from the area Judd and Vicki would need to travel.

"We got 'em now!" the commander shouted.

The chopper flew overhead, its lights filling the sky. Lionel wondered how Conrad had gotten Phoenix to bark like that.

Judd counted down the minutes. Vicki nervously paced in front of the opening.

"It's time," Judd said.

"You go first," Vicki said, helping Judd up to the ledge that led to the opening.

As he reached back to help Vicki up, the earth trembled. The concrete wall he was standing on swayed. A large beam fell, and with it came bricks and mortar.

Vicki let go of Judd's hand and fell back. Judd was thrown forward, outside the church. As quickly as the aftershock had started, it was over, but the hole Judd had crawled through was blocked by debris.

Judd whispered Vicki's name, but she didn't respond. He grabbed handfuls of dirt and rocks and pulled bricks from the opening. He felt like he was clawing for his life.

When the hole was big enough, he stuck his head through. He whispered again, and this time he heard a faint coughing coming from the floor.

"Vick, can you hear me?"

"There's something on my leg," Vicki choked.

"Hang on. I'll get you out!"

"No," Vicki said. "This is your chance. Go!"

"If you think I'm leaving you now, you're crazy," Judd said, frantically moving debris from the entrance.

"Even if you could get me out—"

"Save your breath," Judd said. "I'm almost through." He carefully squeezed through the hole. "I can't see you, Vick. Talk to me."

"I can't move my right leg at all," Vicki said.

Judd felt along the mound of dirt until he touched Vicki's hand.

"I got you now," Judd said, pulling at the dirt and rocks. A few minutes later only the beam trapped her.

"I have to get some leverage to get you out," Judd said. He found a stick outside and brought it in, but it broke in half when he tried to move the beam.

"Time's running out," Vicki said.

"Hang in there. I've almost got it."

The tree branch lifted the beam, and Vicki managed to slide backward before it fell. Vicki got up and hobbled toward the entrance. "I can't put any weight on my leg," she said.

Judd climbed outside and pulled Vicki through. Judd felt her ankle.

Vicki winced. "That's it."

"It doesn't feel broken," Judd said. "But it's bad."

"Let me see if I can walk on it again."

Vicki stood but crumpled to the ground in pain. "It's no use. I can't go."

"I'll carry you," Judd said.

"I'll slow you down."

"I'm telling you, I'm not leaving you."

As Judd lifted Vicki into his arms, he heard the sound of the chopper, then footsteps nearby. He reached for his rear pocket and felt for Conrad's gun. It was still there.

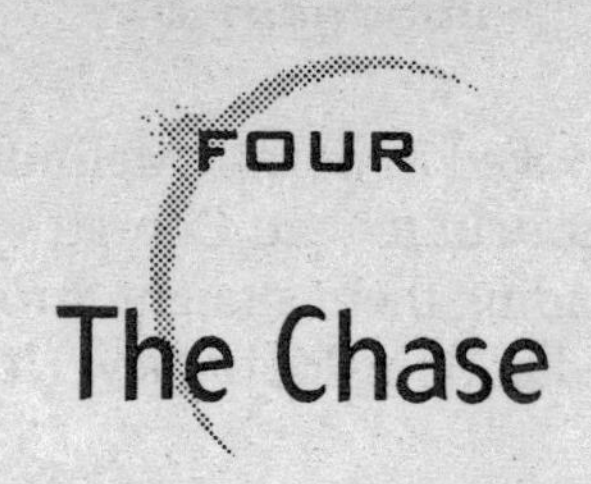

FOUR

The Chase

LIONEL ran with Melinda and Felicia toward the chopper. The earth tremor answered his question about Phoenix. The dog was going wild because of the shudder of the earth. Lionel hoped Judd and Vicki had gotten out of the church.

The radio was busy with reports about the quake. Commander Blancka said, "Keep going and find them. I'll join the chopper." He gave his location and asked the pilot to pick him up.

Melinda led the group with a flashlight and a global positioning device the commander had given her.

"Where are you going?" Lionel said.

"Conrad should be due north if my GPS is right," Melinda said.

Lionel looked in horror. Melinda was taking a shortcut toward Conrad's position. She was leading them straight through the demolished parking lot of New Hope Village Church.

Judd had carried Vicki only a few yards when he saw the beam of the flashlight and heard voices. It sounded like Lionel, but someone was with him. Judd ran to a fallen tree and placed Vicki on the other side. He tried not to breathe.

"How much farther?" a girl said.

"About half a mile," another girl said.

The three Morale Monitors passed a few feet on the other side of the downed tree. Judd heard Lionel say, "I hope that after-shock didn't damage the shelters."

When the three passed, Vicki tried to walk but stumbled in pain. "I don't want you to have to carry me all the way to the Stahley place."

"You're light," Judd said. "It's not a problem."

But Judd knew Vicki was right. No matter how light she was, he couldn't carry her that distance. As he ducked in and out of crumpled subdivisions, he frantically looked for a bike, a motorcycle, or anything that would help them get away. After ten minutes, Judd put Vicki down and fell to his knees, exhausted.

"You can't do this," Vicki said. "Leave me here and come back later."

"No way," Judd said. "Just let me catch my breath."

Lionel knew they needed to give Judd and Vicki as much time as possible. As they topped a hill, the helicopter's searchlight scanned a row of houses.

"There he is!" Melinda shouted, pointing at Conrad.

Conrad held Phoenix by the collar. Commander Blancka had just arrived. Phoenix growled and barked at the man when he came close.

"All right, where'd you see them?" the commander said.

"I saw two people in there," Conrad said, pointing to a small, white house a few yards away. "The dog was going crazy."

"Did you see them run in or come out?" the commander said.

"No, sir, they were moving around inside."

"Then we've got 'em!" The commander barked orders to the chopper. It trained its searchlight on the house as the others took position.

Suddenly, the door opened and a man in his nightclothes walked out. A woman in a robe held a baby. The man put his hands up and squinted.

"On the ground!" the commander shouted through a bullhorn.

The man fell to the ground and put his hands behind his head. The woman came outside and sat beside him with the crying baby. The commander waved the chopper away.

"We didn't do anything," the man said.

"Is that them?" the commander shouted.

"No!" Melinda shouted.

"Maybe they're inside," Lionel said.

The woman cried and shook her head. "Someone flashed a light in our bedroom window, then we felt the earthquake."

"Search it," Commander Blancka yelled.

Lionel followed the others inside. He knew Judd and Vicki hadn't been there.

"I thought I saw them, sir," Conrad said. "The dog went wild, and—"

"Don't think anymore!" the commander said. "Let the dog loose."

Conrad let go of Phoenix's collar. Phoenix sat. The commander kicked at him and yelled, "Go find your friends!"

Phoenix dodged the commander's boot,

and the man lost his balance and fell. Phoenix ran into the night. The chopper followed with its searchlight. Phoenix sniffed at the ground and headed back toward the church.

Judd found that carrying Vicki over his shoulder made running easier. She said she didn't mind, but Judd knew the jostling couldn't be comfortable.

Judd passed a house with a four-wheel-drive vehicle parked in front. A light was on in the living room, and Judd spotted someone sitting in a chair.

"Just act like you've passed out," Judd told Vicki.

"A few more minutes and I won't have to act," Vicki said.

Judd kicked at the door. "Hello? I need help!"

Judd peered through a broken windowpane. A man walked into the front hallway.

"Hi. My friend was hurt in the aftershock, and I was wondering—"

"Go away," the man said.

"I need to get her some help!"

The living room light went out. Judd reached inside the broken window.

"What are you doing?" Vicki whispered.

"Looking for a key to that car," Judd said.

When he couldn't find the key, he carried Vicki down the street. Two blocks later he spotted a crumpled bicycle with something attached behind it.

"It's one of those kid carriers," Vicki said.

"It might work," Judd said.

Judd quickly unhooked the carrier. Vicki fit in the stroller, but she had to keep her feet in the air. Judd pushed her a few yards but noticed the front wheel was bent. The ground was so uneven that Judd abandoned the idea and picked Vicki up again.

"Do you know where we are?" Vicki said.

A dog came at them. Judd kicked at it and kept moving. "About a third of the way there. If we can make it by daylight, we've got a chance."

Lionel had to make a tough decision. If he let Phoenix continue, the dog would lead them straight to Judd and Vicki. He thought of shooting Phoenix. It would keep his friends safe a little while longer.

What am I thinking? Lionel thought. *I can't shoot Phoenix, no matter what.*

Lionel caught up with Conrad. "Nice try."

"I thought that might hold them off longer," Conrad said. "It was murder trying to find a house with somebody in it and hold that dog back at the same time. What do we do now?"

"Hang back and see how this plays out. Judd and Vicki might get away. If the worst happens and they get caught, we can pull our guns on the GC."

"You forgot," Conrad said. "I don't have a gun. Judd got mine."

"If you have to, disarm Melinda or Felicia. Take them by surprise."

"Do you really want to take on Blancka like that?" Conrad said. "I'm through with the GC myself, but there's no way you can work from the inside if you pull a gun."

The chopper followed Phoenix through the twisted wreckage. Phoenix kept his nose to the ground and darted through the rubble. Without the chopper it would have been impossible to keep up with him.

A call from headquarters came over the radio. Someone had just reported two prowlers running through the neighborhood west of New Hope Village Church. Commander Blancka asked for the exact location and got it. He instructed the chopper pilot to abandon the dog and go for the prowlers.

Judd kept moving. He jogged through backyards and parking lots. He looked for grass. The roads were terrible. Huge chunks of asphalt heaved up.

Dogs were not an enemy, but they seemed so spooked at the aftershock that every one of them barked. More than once Judd stumbled and nearly fell. He hit his head on a low-hanging tree limb, and Vicki's clothes got caught in the branches.

Then the sound Judd feared most. The chopper.

Judd saw light a short distance away and ran toward it. He knelt in the grass a few yards from a series of tents.

"It's another shelter," Vicki said, as Judd gasped for breath.

"The chopper's right behind us. If we don't figure out a better way to get around than this, we're sunk."

"Maybe we can buy some time if we hide in there," Vicki said.

Judd felt the beating of chopper blades, and the wind picked up.

Lionel met with Conrad while they waited for orders from Commander Blancka.

Conrad took Lionel's flashlight and turned it on his own face.

"See anything new?" Conrad said.

Lionel shook his head. "What?"

"Don't you see anything right here?" Conrad said, pointing to his forehead.

Lionel smiled. "All right, brother! Good to have you on board."

Vicki hopped to the rear of the tent and fell to the ground. She scooted under the edge and held the flap for Judd. There was little light inside.

"Feels creepy in here," Vicki whispered.

Judd put a finger to his lips.

When her eyes got accustomed to the darkness of the room, Vicki gasped. "Nobody's going to hear us in here. They're all dead."

Sheets draped the bodies around the room. By the size of the bodies Vicki could tell some were young, others older.

"I bet we're near the high school," Vicki said. "This has to be the morgue."

Judd shuddered. "Sorry."

"It's perfect," Vicki said. "Nobody to rat on us."

The chopper hovered over the shelter. People ran from tents and scrambled out of sleeping bags. A car drove up a few yards away.

"I want all of these tents searched," a man yelled. "Washington, you two check here. You two, that tent."

An older woman shouted, "What's going on here?"

"Commander Blancka, Global Community. We're looking for two suspects."

"Everyone in camp is registered," the woman said. "Would you like to see the records?"

"No, ma'am," Commander Blancka said. "We're gonna eyeball every person here to make sure."

Vicki looked at Judd. The tent flap opened.

"That's the morgue," the woman said.

"Ick," a girl said. "I'm not goin' in there."

"Washington," Commander Blancka said, "you check the morgue."

Lionel lifted a few sheets and looked at the faces of the dead. He shook his head and was about to leave when he heard hissing.

"Psst, over here!"

"You guys are in deep," Lionel whispered as he grabbed two sheets at the front of the tent and handed them to Judd and Vicki. Judd explained the situation.

"You can't stay here," Lionel said. "They'll be taking the bodies out of here in the morning."

"Think we can get the commander's jeep?" Judd said.

Lionel smirked. "Oh, that would be too cool. But there's no way."

"If you could create one more diversion, I might be able to get it."

"But the chopper'd be on you in a second," Lionel said.

"It's worth a shot, don't you think?" Judd said.

The tent flap opened and two men came in carrying a body. Lionel covered Judd and Vicki and stood.

"Another stiff to check out?" Lionel said.

The men didn't answer. They put the body down, covered it, and left.

"OK," Lionel said. "Here's what I'll do."

The helicopter circled the camp with its light still on. Lionel approached the commander slowly. Melinda and Felicia were searching tents nearby.

"Sir, I found something kind of strange in the morgue," Lionel said loudly enough for everyone to hear. "I wonder if you'd take a look."

Lionel led the group into the tent and took

them to the side where Judd and Vicki had entered.

"I found one of the tent pegs out and these two sheets."

"I'll bet they crawled in here and pretended to be dead," Melinda said.

"Good call," the commander said.

"Sir, I wasn't able to search all these bodies. I think we ought to do that now."

Commander Blancka lifted the two sheets. He pulled the edge of the tent up and cursed. "My jeep! They're in my jeep!"

FIVE

The River

WHEN Judd got the jeep rolling, he handed the microphone to Vicki and said, "Push this and hold it. It'll jam the frequency of the pilot. Then keep quiet."

Vicki keyed the microphone just in time. The jeep was barely past the morgue when Vicki saw Commander Blancka and the others rush out.

Vicki tapped Judd on the shoulder and pointed behind them. Judd nodded, pointed to the microphone, and gave Vicki a thumbs-up.

Judd drove onto roads he would never have thought were passable. The jeep rolled up embankments and over downed power lines. He kept the car going toward the Stahley mansion, zigging and zagging past collapsed buildings and burned-out cars. The helicopter remained over the shelter. Judd looked at the gas gauge. The tank was almost empty.

Lionel watched a frantic Commander Blancka try to contact the pilot. Blancka called several times but got no response. The man ripped the radio from his shoulder in disgust. "They're jamming us! Somebody get his attention!"

The man waved his arms. Melinda and Felicia joined in, shouting and yelling.

Conrad rolled his eyes and pulled Lionel aside. "You know where I stand with you guys. Now that I'm one of you, there's no way I can stay inside the GC."

"Why not?"

"It's clear what's ahead. We're coming down to the end. Just a little more than five years and the game's up, right?"

"Sure, but what's that got to do—"

"We're looking at one huge countdown clock," Conrad said. "I'm choosing sides now, and it's not with the GC."

"But choosing sides doesn't mean you leave your friends when they're in trouble," Lionel said.

"I don't want to leave them, but—"

"If it were just you and me," Lionel said, "I'd be out of here in a second. But I'm thinking about Judd and Vicki."

"All right. But when we know they're safe, I'm gone."

The girls waved wildly at the chopper. Melinda finally made it to the searchlight and pointed toward the camp. The chopper turned.

"It won't be long now," Lionel said. "I hope Judd's far enough away to ditch the jeep and make it on foot."

Judd drove fast, twisting and winding through the churned-up roads. A few spots had already been repaired by GC crews, and on those Judd was able to make good time. But most roads were like a giant jigsaw puzzle that had been shaken apart.

Vicki tightly wrapped a rag around the microphone and put it under the seat.

"How much gas do we have left?" she said.

"Not much," Judd said. "They've probably made contact with the chopper by now."

"Do you know where you're going?" Vicki said.

"I know the right direction," Judd said. "Don't recognize these roads, though."

They came to an intersection littered with debris. Judd drove around it until he came to a house in the middle of the street. "Cover your head," he said.

"You're not actually going through there, are you?" Vicki said.

Judd floored it and broke through the brittle wall and out the other side.

Vicki threw pieces of wood from the jeep. "I know where we are now," she said. "This is how I came back after leaving Mrs. Jenness."

Judd rolled over two yellow bumps, and Vicki told him it was all that was left of a fast-food restaurant.

"The river's that way," Vicki said.

When Judd crested the hill he couldn't believe his eyes. Twisted pieces of metal were all that was left of the bridge. The road ended at the edge of the river.

"How did you ever survive that?" Judd said.

Vicki shook her head. The memory of her ordeal with Mrs. Jenness was fresh.

"If I'm right, the river runs through the forest preserve," Judd said. "That means we're not far. That's the good news."

"And the bad news?"

"The Stahley place is on the other side of the river. We're going to have to find a way across."

"There's probably not a bridge within miles that survived the quake," Vicki said.

"Then we'll have to swim. Or get a boat."

Vicki turned in horror. "Look!"

The chopper hovered in the distance, its searchlight darting across the road. Judd stopped the jeep. "Quick," he said, "get under what's left of the bridge!"

"I'll try," Vicki said. She hobbled out and headed for the riverbank.

Judd turned the jeep around, unwrapped the rag from the microphone, and pushed in the cigarette lighter. He unscrewed the gas cap and stuffed the rag into the hole. He looked for a stick or a piece of wood long enough and finally found a tire iron behind the backseat.

Judd checked the sky. The chopper was closing ground. He looked back and saw that Vicki was almost hidden.

I hope there's enough gas in there! he thought.

When the lighter was red-hot, Judd lit the rag. He wedged the tire iron against the accelerator and put the jeep in gear. He hoped the car would travel a good distance from the river before it overturned, but it only went a few hundred feet before the front wheels turned and the jeep ran straight into a demolished house. Seconds later an explosion rocked the street. The jeep burst into flames.

Judd ran from the wreck as the chopper flew near.

Lionel stayed close to the commander and listened for news from the pilot. The commander had gone to a different radio frequency, and the chopper immediately pursued the jeep.

"We've got something here, Commander," the pilot said a few minutes later.

"Go ahead."

"An explosion. I'm just getting to the site now. Yeah, it looks like it's your vehicle. It crashed into a house. It's on fire, sir."

"Put down as close as you can and see if those two are in there," the commander said.

"If they are, they're toast," the pilot said. "I don't see any bodies outside the building."

Lionel glanced at Conrad. Conrad shook his head. Melinda and Felicia looked excited.

Vicki couldn't see the chopper, but she heard it and tasted dust. The pain in her leg was so great she had to concentrate on putting one foot in front of the other as Judd helped her move along the side of the river.

"Why'd you blow it up?"

"Thought about sending it into the river," Judd said, "but I figured it was better they find it burning. Might give us a few more minutes to run."

"This is not running," Vicki said.

"You're doing fine," Judd said.

"Any chance they might think we're dead?"

"I hope so," Judd said. "It'll take a while to sift through the wreckage. How's the ankle?"

"Hurts," Vicki said, "but you were right about the sprain. If it was broken, I wouldn't be able to walk at all."

The river had changed since Vicki had last seen it. The bank was much steeper. The river was wider and swollen. In places, the earth had shifted, creating small waterfalls. The water looked much too swift to swim.

"How much farther?" Vicki said.

"Maybe a mile or two."

Judd moved to the edge of the water, then returned. "Too deep to cross. Keep moving."

Vicki saw whitecaps in the moonlight as the river rushed past. Pieces of the bank were still crumbling into the water.

"Look at that," Judd said, pointing to the middle of the river.

Vicki saw a front porch sticking out of the water, being swept downstream. The white picket fence on the porch was still attached, but the rest of the house was underwater and rolling. When it reached the first waterfall, the house hung on the edge, then with a sickening crunch, crashed over the side and broke apart.

It was difficult to walk along the churned-up ground. Vicki slipped several times and had to be helped to her feet. "Let's move to the top of the bank," she said.

"We'll be too easy to spot up there," Judd said.

"If he's got night vision, it won't matter," Vicki said. She took another step and her ankle gave way. She plunged down the hill, grabbing at dirt and grass as she tumbled. But she couldn't hang on. With fistfuls of dirt, she splashed into the chilly water.

Lionel heard the call from the pilot and rushed to the commander's side.

"Go ahead," the commander said.

"Heat's pretty intense here, sir. I don't

see any bodies inside or out. Looks staged."

"Those vehicles don't just burst into flames," the commander said. "Continue the search. We've got a second chopper on the way to help you."

Judd heard Vicki cry out. He turned as she flipped and rolled down the embankment. A splash. Vicki was in the churning water.

Judd scampered down the hill. His foot caught on a tree root and he, too, tumbled headfirst into the water. The current was swift and took him under. He surfaced and yelled for Vicki, but she didn't answer. Then a strange sound mixed with the gurgling water in Judd's ears. It was the *thwock, thwock, thwock* of the helicopter.

For a moment, Judd felt a sense of relief. The GC chopper could rescue them. But Judd knew once he was in the hands of the GC, he and Vicki would be separated and probably punished.

The chopper darted over the water, the blades whipping up waves and making the swimming harder. It flew from bank to bank. Judd went under and stayed as long as his lungs could stand it.

Vicki was underwater for what seemed an eternity. She didn't have time to take a breath when she fell in. The current pushed her downstream into the roots of a tree. The water was black and icy. She struggled to get free, breaking a branch that snagged her clothes, but soon she was caught on another. Finally, the current took her away from the tree, and she rose to the surface.

Vicki gasped for air. She grabbed for the bank, but it was too far away. The swirling water took her under again. When she surfaced, she called out for Judd.

Vicki's cry was close. Judd turned and saw her shadow against the searchlight. This was their chance.

Judd swam with all his might, and the current pushed Vicki toward him. He screamed and reached out for her.

Judd touched her hand once, then took two more strokes to get closer. *Just a little more,* he thought.

As he strained toward Vicki, a piece of the splintered house hit him and forced him underwater. When he surfaced, he barely heard Vicki's cry above the noise.

Vicki screamed for Judd, then lost sight of him. A bright light blinded her as the water kicked up around her.

"Stay where you are," a voice boomed overhead.

Like I can control where I'm going, Vicki thought.

Out of control, Judd twisted and turned in the river. He tried to swim to shore, but just as he felt he was making progress, the current pulled him under.

When he surfaced, a section of roof hurtled toward him. He couldn't dodge it, and it was too big to swim under, so Judd grabbed the edge and tried to crawl on. As he did, he sent shingles plopping into the water. Finally, Judd made it to the center of the spinning roof.

Where's Vicki? he thought. He didn't know which was worse—being found by the GC or being at the mercy of the river.

He spotted the chopper hovering near the spot where they had fallen in. Judd kicked himself for not being more careful. If only they had walked farther up the bank. If only he had held on to Vicki.

The roof spun completely around, and water washed over him. When Judd could see again, he noticed a rescue line dangling from the chopper. The pilot was shouting something through his loudspeaker. "Don't get on, Vick!" Judd screamed.

Vicki went under and swam toward the shore, but the current was too swift. The chopper hovered closer and dropped a lifeline.

"This is the Global Community!" the pilot shouted. "You are under arrest. Grab the harness and put it around you."

Vicki went under again and kicked as hard as she could. Swimming was easier than walking, but her ankle felt like it was on fire. When she surfaced, the pilot moved into position.

"Grab the harness," the pilot said. "This is your only chance. There's a huge waterfall around the next corner. You don't want to go over that. Grab on and I'll pull you up."

What about Judd? Vicki thought.

"No!" Judd shouted as he watched the chopper pull Vicki from the water. He slammed his fist on the roof of the house and rolled off. When Vicki was in, the chopper flew slowly toward Judd. Before he was spotted,

Judd dove underneath the floating roof. He found a pocket of air and stayed there until the chopper passed.

The roof picked up speed. When Judd surfaced, he thought the chopper was back. But this wasn't the sound of rotor blades. This was a roar. He swam against the current and watched in horror as the roof of the house disappeared over the edge of a chasm.

SIX

Over the Edge

LIONEL stiffened when he heard the pilot's voice.

"We've apprehended one of them," the pilot said. "We have a female in custody. Search for the male is negative. I think he might have drowned."

"Bring the girl back and keep going," Commander Blancka said from the other chopper. "Morale Monitors on the ground, the GC has taken over police headquarters on Maple Street. I want the two girls to head this up. Get everything you can out of her."

Lionel clicked his microphone. "What do you want Graham and me to do, sir?"

"Stay where you are. We'll pick you up."

"This changes everything," Lionel said to Conrad. "Vicki will have no hope unless we help her."

"I'm no chicken, but I'm not a hero either," Conrad said. "And if Vicki's at this police station halfway across town, what are we supposed to do?"

"I don't know yet," Lionel said. "But there's no way I'm letting Blancka decide her fate."

"What about Judd?" Conrad said. "You think he's still alive?"

Lionel hesitated. "Judd'll be all right. He can take care of himself."

Judd tried to swim against the current but couldn't. With nothing to hold on to he took a deep breath, held out his arms, and plunged over the fall into the darkness.

He hit the surface with his feet, and water surrounded him. He sank deeper and deeper. He was afraid he would black out and drown from the fall. With his lungs nearly bursting, he reached the soft bottom and tried to push up. His feet stuck in the muck. Judd struggled and finally kicked free. He rose to the surface and gasped for air.

The water was calm now. The current carried him slowly downriver. Judd found a piece of wood and clung to it with his remaining strength.

Judd watched the riverbank for anything

familiar. After a half hour of drifting, he let go of the wood and swam to shore. He climbed through the mud to the top of the bank. Something slick passed him.

Snake.

A chill went through him, and he clawed his way to the top. Judd tried to get his bearings. He knew he had to go west to get to the Stahley place, but which way was west? The stars were brilliant in the sky. Since the earthquake, they seemed brighter. Without the haze from the city, Judd found the North Star easily.

Once again Judd heard the helicopter. He ran. This time it would be looking for his body.

They're not going to find it, Judd thought as he took off into the forest.

Vicki shook from the cold as she hobbled into the police station. Commander Blancka led the way into the interrogation room. Melinda and Felicia followed.

"Young lady, I'm going to give you a chance," the commander began. "If you cooperate, that'll be taken into consideration when it comes time to sentence you."

Vicki said nothing.

"If you refuse to cooperate, refuse to give us information, I'll have no choice but to be severe with my punishment." The commander looked at Vicki without emotion. "And I can be severe."

After the commander left, Melinda said, "We know your name is Vicki Byrne. Why did you kill Mrs. Jenness?"

"I didn't kill her," Vicki said. "I told you that."

"We have witnesses."

"You have one person who says she thinks she saw something. It won't stand up."

Melinda smiled. "You don't understand. This isn't a court. There won't be a trial. Whatever Commander Blancka decides is final."

"I have a right to a fair—"

"You lost your rights when you disobeyed the Global Community," Felicia said. "They could have left you in the water to die. Or shot you for stealing GC property. If the commander decides you murdered that lady, he's told us what will happen."

"And what's that?" Vicki said.

Melinda leaned close. "Death."

Judd huddled in a thicket of bushes. The chopper stayed near the river.

The forest had felt the effects of the earthquake just as the city had. Trees were uprooted. Whole sections of the forest had been swallowed. Judd recognized what was left of the access road and ran toward a meadow. He found the small grove of trees where he had knelt with Ryan and Taylor Graham. Judd found the remote entry box and pushed the button. He glanced at the hill. Nothing happened. He pushed the button again. Still, nothing happened.

Judd looked around for any sign of the GC. He couldn't see the house, but he assumed it was deserted. Both Mr. and Mrs. Stahley were dead. There was no reason to guard it unless they were still looking for Darrion.

Judd ran to the door built into the hill. He tried to find an opening, but the shifting ground had sealed the entrance. Digging would take hours.

He walked around the meadow and onto the Stahley property. The huge fence that surrounded the property was on the ground. The security gate at the front of the property was also in shambles. Judd hoped the earthquake had scared off the dogs.

Judd climbed through broken glass on the patio area. The swimming pool was empty.

Judd leaned over and saw a huge crack in the bottom of the pool. The roof had collapsed over the kitchen, but the house hadn't been damaged like many Judd had seen.

Looters had been there. The refrigerator was open, food strewn around the kitchen. The high-tech television and stereo equipment were gone from the living room.

With the sun coming up, Judd felt exhausted. He wanted to see the hideout downstairs. If the equipment was still there, and if the phone lines were up, he might be able to contact others in the Trib Force. Someone had to help Vicki.

Judd put his head down on the couch. *I'll just lie down for a moment,* he thought.

As soon as he put his head down, he was asleep.

Though the commander ordered him to stay, Lionel left to find Darrion and Shelly. He found them sleeping at a nearby shelter. He woke them and explained what had happened to Vicki.

"What about Judd?" Shelly said.

"We don't know," Lionel said. "We hope he got away. There's a chance he could have drowned."

Shelly shook her head.

"We have to help Vicki," Darrion said. "Is there any way to hire a lawyer or have someone negotiate for her?"

"It's worth a shot," Lionel said. "Commander Blancka has full power from the Global Community. He's the judge and jury."

"Who could we get?" Shelly said. "I don't know any lawyers."

"What about Mr. Stein?" Darrion said. "Vicki said he offered to help any way he could."

Lionel told Shelly and Darrion to get Mr. Stein. If they couldn't find him, they were to go to Darrion's house. As soon as Vicki's case was settled, the remaining members of the Young Tribulation Force would meet there.

Judd awoke at noon, hungry and aching. He stumbled to the kitchen and found an unopened box of crackers. That eased his hunger for a while. He hoped the earthquake hadn't damaged the secret entrance to the underground hangar.

He found a picture of the Stahleys hanging at a weird angle. He pried the secret entrance open and crawled onto the landing behind the wall. The ladder that led to the secret room had fallen, so Judd scampered back to the kitchen and found a piece of rope. He climbed into darkness and activated the entrance.

Inside the chamber Judd found the safe still open. He had taken the secret documents but left gold coins and a stack of bills. The door to the safe was still open, and the money and gold were gone. He pulled Ryan's packet from his pocket, still damp, and placed it inside the safe.

Judd checked the hangar for the stash of food Taylor Graham had shown him. It was still there. He went back to the computer room and picked up the phone. Dial tone. That meant he could access the Internet.

A few minutes later he was viewing Rabbi Tsion Ben-Judah's Web site. Judd sent an urgent message to the man, hoping he would be able to help with Vicki. While he waited, Judd read the rabbi's latest posting. Thousands of messages had poured in since the earthquake. Many identified themselves as members of the 144,000 Jewish witnesses. An on-screen meter showed the number of responses as they were added to the central bulletin board. The numbers whizzed past.

Judd only wanted to spend a few minutes on the Net, but he couldn't stop reading Dr.

Ben-Judah's message. The main posting was based on Revelation 8 and 9. Tsion believed the wrath of the Lamb earthquake began the second period of the Tribulation. Tsion wrote:

> There are seven years, or eighty-four months, in all. You can see we are now one quarter of the way through. As bad as things have been, they get worse.
>
> What is next? In Revelation 8:5 an angel takes a censer, fills it with fire from the altar of God, and throws it to the earth. That results in noise, thunder, lightning, and an earthquake.
>
> That same chapter goes on to say that seven angels with seven trumpets prepared themselves to sound. That is where we are now. Sometime over the next twenty-one months, the first angel will sound, and hail and fire will follow, mingled with blood, thrown down to the earth. This will burn a third of the trees and all the green grass.

Judd knew he needed to make contact with someone about helping Vicki, but he couldn't stop reading. He was looking at what he would have to experience if he survived.

> Later a second angel will sound the second trumpet, and the Bible says a great mountain burning with fire will be thrown into the sea. This will turn a third of the water to blood, kill a third of the living creatures in the sea, and sink a third of the ships.

Judd was stunned. He shook his head and tried to imagine all those things taking place. The world would be in even greater turmoil than it was now, after the worldwide earthquake. He read on.

> The third angel's trumpet sound will result in a great star falling from heaven, burning like a torch. It will somehow fall over a wide area and land in a third of the rivers and springs. This star is even named in Scripture. The book of Revelation calls it Wormwood. Where it falls, the water becomes bitter and people die from drinking it.

Judd heard a ding and a window popped up saying he had an E-mail. It was Dr. Ben-Judah.

"Judd, I have been praying for you and your friends. Is everyone all right?"

Judd brought Tsion up-to-date and gave

him the bad news about Ryan. There was a long pause.

"I am sorry you have to go through such a painful experience. Losing a friend like Ryan is very difficult. His love for God's Word was an encouragement to me. I will miss him greatly."

"What about the adult Trib Force?" Judd wrote.

"Buck is searching for Chloe even now," Tsion wrote. "Please pray. Rayford is alive in New Babylon. Unfortunately, his wife, Amanda, was on a flight that is reported missing. Rayford still holds out hope that she is alive, but the reports are not encouraging."

"What about Loretta and Donny at the church?"

"They are both in the presence of Jesus," Tsion wrote. "Donny's wife as well."

Judd shook his head. Loretta had been like a second mom to him. He told Tsion about Vicki, and the rabbi said he would stop everything and pray for her.

"O God," Tsion wrote, "you have delivered your servants from the lions, from the furnace, and from the hands of evil authorities. I pray you would deliver our dear sister from any harm now. May your peace wash over her and may she remain faithful to you in every word and action."

Vicki wondered when Melinda and Felicia would tire. She was barely able to keep her eyes open as they asked question after question. Finally, they escorted her to a cell.

Vicki put her head down on a cot. Her ankle was swollen and turning blue, but it didn't hurt as much. Her clothes had dried so she wasn't cold anymore.

She knew she should feel afraid, but she didn't. When she had asked God to forgive her, she didn't know how dangerous that decision would be. Now, if she had to give her life for the cause, she felt OK. Ryan had done it. Bruce had given his life as well.

If God wants me to go through the same thing as them, then so be it, she thought. She closed her eyes and for the first time in days slept soundly.

SEVEN

Pavel's News

JUDD was thrilled to talk with Dr. Ben-Judah. When Judd asked where Tsion was staying, the rabbi replied, "I think it is safer if neither of us knows where the other is."

Tsion signed off. Judd e-mailed Pavel, his friend in New Babylon. Pavel had read Tsion's Web site and talked with Judd about receiving Christ. Judd was grateful this new believer had survived the earthquake. While he waited to make contact, Judd revisited Tsion's Web site. The rabbi wrote:

> How can a thinking person see all that has happened and not fear what is to come? If there are still unbelievers after the third Trumpet Judgment, the fourth should convince everyone. Anyone who resists the warnings of God at that time

> will likely have already decided to serve the enemy. The fourth Trumpet Judgment is a striking of the sun, the moon, and the stars so that a third of the sun, a third of the moon, and a third of the stars are darkened. We will never again see sunshine as bright as we have before. The brightest summer day with the sun high in the sky will be only two-thirds as bright as it ever was. How will this be explained away?

Judd shook his head. "People explained away the fact that Jesus came back from the dead, too," he muttered. He read on with chills. What Tsion was writing would one day come true.

> In the middle of this, the writer of the Revelation says he looked and heard an angel "flying through the midst of heaven." It was saying with a loud voice, "Woe, woe, woe to the inhabitants of the earth, because of the remaining blasts of the trumpet of the three angels who are about to sound!"

Tsion said he would cover more in his next lesson and ended with an encouraging message. The rabbi said he believed there was a time coming when many would believe in Christ. Tsion called it a "great soul harvest." He wrote:

> Consider these promises. In the Old Testament book of Joel 2:28-32, God is speaking. He says, "And it shall come to pass afterward that I will pour out My Spirit on all flesh; your sons and your daughters shall prophesy, your old men shall dream dreams, your young men shall see visions. And also on My menservants and on my maidservants I will pour out My Spirit in those days."

I wonder if that means me? Judd thought. He continued.

> "And I will show wonders in the heavens and in the earth: blood and fire and pillars of smoke. The sun shall be turned into darkness, and the moon into blood, before the coming of the great and awesome day of the Lord.
>
> "And it shall come to pass that whoever calls on the name of the Lord shall be saved. For in Mount Zion and in Jerusalem there shall be deliverance, as the Lord has said, among the remnant whom the Lord calls."

Judd read on. Tsion wrote that Revelation makes it clear that the judgments he mentioned would not come until the servants of God had been sealed on their foreheads.

"That's just happened," Judd said, putting a hand to his forehead.

> We are called by God to be servants. The function of a servant of Christ is to communicate the gospel of the grace of God. Although we will go through great persecution, we can comfort ourselves that during the Tribulation we look forward to astounding events outlined in Revelation.
>
> Revelation 7:9 quotes John saying, "After these things I looked, and behold, a great multitude which no one could number, of all nations, tribes, peoples, and tongues, standing before the throne and before the Lamb, clothed with white robes, with palm branches in their hands. . . ."
>
> These are the tribulation saints. Now follow me carefully. In a later verse, Revelation 9:16, the writer numbers the army of horsemen in a battle at two hundred million. If such a vast army can be numbered, what might the Scriptures mean when they refer to the tribulation

> saints, those who come to Christ during this period, as "a great multitude which no one could number"?

Judd sat back. He saw the logic. God was about to do something incredible on the earth and if he lived, Judd would get to see it.

> Do you see why I believe we are justified in trusting God for more than a billion souls during this period? Let us pray for that great harvest. All who name Christ as their Redeemer can have a part in this, the greatest task ever assigned to mankind.

Vicki awoke. She couldn't tell whether it was morning or evening. The only window was toward the back of the jail area, out of her sight. She had slept soundly and awoke refreshed and hungry. Her ankle was tender, but she could at least stand on it without falling over.

An hour later a GC guard brought her some bread and soup. "Can you tell me what time it is?" Vicki said.

"Almost six," the man said.

"A.M. or P.M.?" Vicki said.

"P.M., miss," the guard said. "And you have a visitor waiting. They're getting him cleared right now."

Vicki couldn't imagine who it was. It couldn't be Judd, unless he was wearing some kind of disguise. A few minutes later Vicki heard the clicking heels of a well-dressed man. The guard opened the door, and the man stood in the shadows. He took off his hat and stepped forward.

Vicki gasped. "Mr. Stein!"

Pavel contacted Judd a few minutes later. Judd brought him up-to-date with all he had been through.

"I'm glad you're safe for now," Pavel wrote. "Many things are happening here as well."

"Like what?" Judd wrote.

"The rebuilding effort is going strong. Thousands are working with Cellular-Solar o get the communications network up. Some are being forced to help rebuild airports."

"Carpathia cares more about people traveling and talking with each other than he does about the sick and dying," Judd wrote. "The people at the shelters are doing the best they can. That's where the relief effort should be going."

"You are right," Pavel wrote, "though everyone here has been glowing about how Nicolae is handling the disaster. They talk of him as if he were a god. In fact, that may be what he thinks he is."

Judd sat forward. "What do you mean?"

"My father survived the quake. He said strange things about Nicolae. There are people who believe he is more than human."

Mr. Stein smiled. The guard would not allow him inside the cell. Instead, he sat on a stool outside.

"How are you?"

"Considering I almost drowned, I'm OK," Vicki said. "How did you know I was here?"

"A little bird," Mr. Stein said. "No, make that two. They told me what happened and that you were in trouble."

"That's an understatement," Vicki said. "Are you a lawyer?"

"No, but I know enough about the legal process to help. I would contact one of my lawyer friends, but I'm not sure there is time."

"Why?"

"This commander who will make the decision about you seems to have made up his mind. I told him I wanted to represent you, and he asked why I would bother. He seems very anxious to move ahead."

"Which means what?" Vicki said.

"If there is any arguing or convincing that will be done, it has to be done now."

"And you're going to try?"

"Unless you have another idea."

Vicki shook her head.

"First, you must tell me if you are guilty of the charge of murder."

Vicki explained what had happened with Mrs. Jenness. Mr. Stein listened intently and took a few notes. He scratched his chin when Vicki told about trying to pull Mrs. Jenness from the sinking car.

"This woman was your enemy," Mr. Stein said. "She was against you and those you were working with."

"I didn't really see her as an enemy," Vicki said. "She didn't know the truth. I always hoped we would someday be able to break through to her. That's what I was trying to do when the earthquake hit. I was telling her that Jesus is—"

"Enough," Mr. Stein said. "I know your position by heart. Now tell me this: Why would you go back to help her? If you had saved her, she would have handed you over to the Global Community."

"A person's life is worth a lot more than my comfort or safety," Vicki said. "I tried to help her because she needed it. Sure, she could have turned me in, but if I hadn't tried, I couldn't live with myself."

Mr. Stein frowned. "I'm asking these questions because this is what the commander will ask. You're saying you helped Mrs. Jenness because . . . "

"There's a verse in the Bible that says there's no greater love than for a person to lay down his life for a friend," Vicki said.

"But she wasn't your friend," Mr. Stein said.

"Exactly," Vicki said. "And I wasn't a friend of Jesus when he gave his life for me. I was sinful and against him, and he still died for me."

"So you used that example to give you the strength to help Mrs. Jenness."

Vicki hung her head. "I only wish it would have worked."

Mr. Stein leaned forward. "I can't lie to you. When I talked to the commander and the young ladies he employs, they were rounding up the witnesses who say you actually murdered this woman."

"They have a girl who hates me and would say anything to get me in trouble, and they have another lady who saw me on the bridge in Mrs. Jenness's car."

"I admit the evidence is slim, but it is your word against the two of them. And Mrs. Jenness is dead. Is there anyone you can think of who could testify on your behalf?"

"Anyone I'd ask would be in bigger trouble because of it," Vicki said, leaning forward. "I want you to know, if I had it to do over again, I'd take the same chance. I don't care what happens. They can lock me up if they want."

"It will be much worse than that," Mr. Stein said.

Someone knocked on the door and motioned for the guard.

"Let me do the talking," Mr. Stein said.

Judd shuddered. "Are you sure no one can trace this?"

"I'm sure," Pavel said. "I'm using a line my father had installed that cannot be accessed. When I am done, I take my computer back to my room."

"All right," Judd said. "What are the people in the inner circle saying about Nicolae?"

"Leon Fortunato, Carpathia's right-hand man, says he thinks the potentate could be the Messiah."

Judd blinked at the screen. "What does he base that on?"

"Fortunato thinks that because he was raised from the dead, Carpathia has to be some sort of deity."

"And what does Nicolae say about it?"

"He doesn't confirm it or deny it," Pavel said. "My father overheard one of Nicolae's conversations. The potentate said it was not time to make the claim that he is the Messiah, but he wasn't sure it was untrue."

"He thinks he's the Messiah, the savior of the world?"

"He said he knows there are people who say he is *the* Antichrist. He would love to prove them wrong."

"What does your father think?" Judd said.

"He looks at what Nicolae Carpathia has accomplished and says he wouldn't be surprised if Nicolae was sent by God."

Judd shook his head. "And what do you think?"

"I believe there is the one true Messiah and Savior," Pavel wrote, "and that man is Jesus Christ. Nicolae Carpathia is our enemy."

The guard opened the cell door. Melinda led Vicki and Mr. Stein into a conference room.

"When will we be able—," Mr. Stein said, but Melinda waved a hand.

"You can talk with the commander when he gets here," she said.

Vicki waited nervously, then closed her eyes.

"Are you tired?" Mr. Stein asked.

"I'm praying."

Mr. Stein sighed. "I think you had better do more than that."

"There's nothing more powerful I can do," Vicki said. "For some reason God wants me to go through this. I don't know why."

"Why would God want you to be jailed or killed for something you did not do?"

Vicki thought for a moment. *Maybe that's it.*

"In the New Testament there were many people who were killed or sent before authorities," Vicki said. "God said he would give them the right words to say. Maybe the commander or those two girls need to hear the message. Maybe one of them will be used by God to do something great for him."

"You need to be thinking of yourself," Mr. Stein said.

"I thought of myself my whole life," Vicki said. "That got me left behind."

Commander Blancka came in and glared at Vicki.

EIGHT

The Hearing

VICKI watched the commander carefully. He didn't look capable of kindness. His voice was low and gravelly.

"I'll review the charges, then you'll have a chance to respond," the commander muttered. "But this is not a trial. Under the Global Community statute during states of emergency, I'm the judge, the jury, and the one who will pass sentence."

Vicki nodded. Mr. Stein put a hand on her shoulder.

"Vicki Byrne, you're charged with the murder of Mrs. Laverne Jenness. You're also charged with stealing and then destroying Global Community property. You won't give us information on an escapee of a GC reeducation camp, a person whose name is Judd Thompson. That means you're harboring a criminal and subject to the same penalty as the accused.

"You're also charged with crimes against the Global Community and a number of smaller charges—"

"What crimes?" Mr. Stein interrupted.

Commander Blancka looked up. "You will not interrupt me!" he said. "Who are you anyway?"

"My name is Mitchell Stein. Vicki is a friend of the family. I am here to help in her defense."

"As I said, this is not a trial."

"Call it what you will, sir, but your decision will greatly affect my friend's life. She deserves representation."

"We'll find out what she deserves," the commander said. "I have statements from three people. One says Vicki was the last person seen with Mrs. Jenness before her body was found. Another woman says Vicki was seen on the roof pushing Mrs. Jenness inside the car."

Vicki shook her head.

"And the third witness says he helped Vicki dispose of a dead body."

"Commander," Mr. Stein said, "I think it would be helpful to hear Vicki's side of the story."

"I've read her statement," the commander

said. "It's her word against the others. The fact that she ran from us, stole our vehicle, then destroyed it, and that she's been charged with speech against the Global Community in the past is pretty strong evidence, don't you think?"

Mr. Stein cleared his throat. "I am concerned that you do not have the entire story. Surely, if you are going to decide whether such serious charges are true, you should hear from the accused rather than what someone else said."

Vicki looked at Melinda and Felicia. Both girls scowled.

"Vicki is a young woman of faith," Mr. Stein continued. "This is something the Global Community has encouraged."

"The GC hasn't encouraged anyone to commit murder," the commander fumed.

"And if you will hear Vicki out, I think you'll conclude that murder was the last thing on her mind that day. She has a heart of compassion, not murder."

"All right," the commander said. "She can speak."

Judd heard a noise upstairs and muted his computer speakers. Someone was inside the house. *Could be GC, could be burglars,* Judd thought.

Moments later someone climbed down the rope to the secret entrance. Judd looked for a weapon to defend himself, then hit the light switch. The ceiling moved. Judd flipped on the light. It was Darrion and Shelly.

Judd welcomed them.

"We've got a surprise," Darrion said, pointing to the opening. "Look who we found."

Mark stuck his head into the room and grinned. "You were going to attack us with a computer keyboard?" He smirked.

"It was the only thing I could find," Judd said, putting the keyboard down. "Thought you might be the GC."

Mark crawled through and gave Judd a hug. "Have you heard from John?"

"Who's John?" Darrion said.

Judd told Darrion about meeting John and Mark at Nicolae High.

"He was away at school when the quake hit," Mark said. "I've looked on every list of dead and injured I can find but I don't know anything for sure yet." Mark paused. "I heard about Ryan. I'm sorry."

Judd nodded and bit his lip. "What happened to you?"

"Long story," Mark said, pulling up a chair. "I was at my aunt's house when it hit. She has a dog that doesn't bark at anything. Too lazy. Well, this thing had him running back and forth in the front room, whining and barking. I figured it out before it hit, but I had a hard time convincing my aunt to follow me outside.

"When the roof in the kitchen started cracking, she believed me. I pulled her out just as the wall buckled. We got down the stairs before they collapsed. Then the whole neighborhood went. It was like trying to walk on concrete water."

"Was your aunt hurt?" Judd said.

"She ran back for the dog in the backyard," Mark said. "Glass from next door hit her in the face and neck. Lots of blood. I grabbed the dog in one arm and held her up with the other."

"Between the attack on the militia base and the earthquake, you've had some pretty close calls," Judd said.

Judd brought them up-to-date on what he knew about the Trib Force. They still hadn't heard if Chloe was alive, or whether Rayford's wife, Amanda, had been on the plane that had crashed during the earthquake.

"I just hope the next people we see coming through that opening are Lionel and Vicki," Judd said.

Lionel listened outside the conference room. He didn't want to go in unless Commander Blancka called him.

"We need to plan for the worst," Lionel said. "If she's convicted, we have to be ready."

"For what?" said Conrad.

"To spring her."

Vicki felt nervous, but Mr. Stein's smile calmed her.

"Vicki, why don't you tell the commander about the morning of the earthquake?"

Vicki nodded. "Mrs. Jenness caught me before school with some papers," she said. "I was trying to warn people about the earthquake."

"Wait," the commander said. "You knew there was going to be an earthquake?"

"It's predicted in the Bible," Vicki said. "I didn't know it was going to hit that morning, but it was the next event that was supposed to happen. I can show you if—"

The commander waved a hand. "No, just go ahead."

"Mrs. Jenness was angry. She destroyed the papers, and we headed toward a GC facility."

"Is it true you spent some time away from school because of a behavior problem?" the commander said, glancing toward Melinda.

"Yes," Vicki admitted. "The school thought I was behind the *Underground* newspaper so I was sent away."

"So you were guilty and trying to hide it?"

"Yes," Vicki said.

"Tell us about what happened on the bridge," Mr. Stein said.

Vicki told them the truth about trying to save Mrs. Jenness's life. When she was through, the commander leaned forward. "You must think I'm crazy," he said. "You actually think I'll believe you tried to save a woman who was trying to put you away?"

Mr. Stein stood. "Commander, I had a hard time believing it myself. Then I took a look at this girl's background. She stayed in our home for a brief time.

"Vicki lost her father, her mother, and her younger sister in the vanishings. The family had gone through some sort of religious awakening. Everyone but Vicki. The disappearances upset her. She couldn't think straight. So she came up with this idea of God taking her family away."

"Wait a minute," Vicki said.

"Quiet, I want to hear this," the commander said.

"To strengthen her belief she began to tell others about it. The more people she told, the more convinced she became it was true. This student newspaper is a good example. She knew it would be a disaster if she were ever caught. But she wanted to spread her message."

"How does this fit with Mrs. Jenness?" the commander said.

"You have to understand her belief," Mr. Stein said. "She thinks Jesus was the Messiah. She bases everything in her life on the notion that Jesus came to take away true believers—and will come again. She lives by his teachings, prays to him, even memorizes the words of the Bible."

Mr. Stein smiled and rummaged through his briefcase. "When I asked her the same question about saving Mrs. Jenness's life, she quoted a verse to me." He flipped open a Bible. Vicki saw it was Chaya's.

"Here it is," he said. "'The greatest love is shown when people lay down their lives for their friends.'"

"And that convinced you she tried to save Mrs. Jenness?" the commander said.

Mr. Stein took off his glasses and walked toward the commander. "Sir, you may call this young lady misguided. You can say she is confused, that her beliefs are wacky, or that she's sick. But her life is controlled by the notion that Mrs. Jenness needed to believe the same way Vicki does to have any hope of heaven."

"And that kind of belief is dangerous to the unity of the Global Community," the commander said.

"You must be the judge of that, sir," Mr. Stein said.

"And I will be."

Vicki stood. "I want to say something."

The commander put his hand to his forehead and squeezed. "Sit!"

"I know what Mr. Stein's trying to do," Vicki said. "He's trying to make it look like I'm mental. I'm not. Take a look around you. People have disappeared. Treaties have been signed. There's been a worldwide earthquake, something the experts said would never happen. All of it was predicted in the Bible. If you ignore this and go on like it hasn't happened, then I say *that's* crazy."

"Do you see what I mean?" Mr. Stein said.

"Stop trying to make me out to be insane!" Vicki shouted.

"Can I have a moment with her, sir?" Mr. Stein said.

Judd grilled Mark about what he had seen.

"Buck Williams is the only person I've seen from the Trib Force," Mark said. "And I only saw him as he passed in his Range Rover."

"So you stayed at shelters?" Judd said.

"I helped my aunt get to one, then a bunch of GC guys came through and loaded anybody healthy onto the back of a truck."

"You must have been scared out of your mind," Shelly said.

"They had no idea who I was," Mark said. "They were just looking for anybody who had the strength to work."

"Let me guess," Judd said. "Cellular-Solar."

"You got it," Mark said. "They worked us all that day and into the night clearing the way for the new communication towers. We cut down old ones and dug holes for new ones. They've got cell towers and satellite receivers just about everywhere."

"How did you get here?" Judd said.

"Saw my chance to run and took off," Mark said. "I came back to check on my aunt and found Shelly and Darrion."

"How's your aunt?" Judd said.

"She'll live, but it'll be a while before I can move her," Mark said.

Lionel stood as Vicki and Mr. Stein walked into the hallway. He had heard most of the conversation and thought the commander might be changing his mind about Vicki.

"You're trying to make me look like a fool," Vicki whispered to Mr. Stein.

"I'm trying to save your life," Mr. Stein said. "Which do you care more about, your reputation or your survival?"

"I don't care what people think about me," Vicki said, "but you're trying to make what I believe look sick."

"If he lets you go, what does it matter?"

"It's not the truth!" Vicki shouted.

Lionel approached. "Vick, it may be a way out for you," he whispered.

"I can't believe you'd go along with this," Vicki said.

"I just want you to get out of here alive."

"And so do I," Mr. Stein said.

The door opened. Melinda and Felicia scowled.

"All right, time for you to get back inside," Lionel barked. He followed them inside.

Melinda whispered something to the commander, then turned and glared at Lionel.

"You have something to say?" the commander said to Mr. Stein.

"Yes," Mr. Stein said with a sheepish look. "Vicki wants to make sure I do not represent her in any way as being sick or crazy."

"Right," the commander said. "Washington!"

Lionel jumped to his feet. "Yes, sir!"

"I'm told you know this girl and her friend who took the jeep."

Sweat rolled down Lionel's forehead. He wiped it away. "Before I went south to the camp I did."

"Have any idea where this Judd Thompson might be?"

"Believe me, sir," Lionel said, "if I knew where Judd was, I'd be there right now."

"Have any comment about this Byrne girl before I decide what to do with her?"

Lionel hesitated. He looked at Vicki. "I don't have any comment, sir, except to say that I know she'll get what she deserves in the end."

Lionel turned and saw a look of surprise on Melinda's face.

The commander shuffled papers and cleared his throat. Before he spoke, a guard entered the room and approached him. The two talked quietly, then the commander hurried to the back door.

"Take her back to her cell," the commander said. "I'll give my decision tomorrow morning. Meet here at 0800 hours."

NINE

The Plan

VICKI was taken to her cell. Mr. Stein followed and was allowed inside.

"What happens now?" Vicki said.

"Your guess is as good as mine," Mr. Stein said. "Sounds like the commander will decide between now and tomorrow morning."

"Do you think there's a chance—?"

"If he believes you are a little off in the head," Mr. Stein said, "he might just send you to a reeducation camp."

"And if not?"

"I don't want to think about it."

"I'm not afraid to die for the gospel," Vicki said.

Mr. Stein shook his head. "I'll never understand why fanatics say things like that. You think it impresses me. It doesn't. There are many people who would give their lives for something foolish."

"The point isn't whether I would die for my faith," Vicki said. "The main thing is whether what I put my faith in is true."

"You sound like my daughter."

"If they said it was illegal to talk about God," Vicki said, "I would die giving you that message. But I'd rather live to see you accept your Messiah. That's what Chaya was praying for all along."

"They're coming for you tomorrow morning," Mr. Stein said, "and the best you can hope for is to go to a reeducation camp. Why would you be concerned about me when you're facing that?"

"Lionel said it best."

"He was against you."

"No, I understood. He said he knew I'd get what I deserved. Because of Jesus, I have the hope of heaven. The Global Community can't take that away."

"I wish I were as confident as you about the future," Mr. Stein said.

Vicki scribbled the address for Tsion Ben-Judah's Web site on a scrap of paper. "Please, when you get home tonight, look this up. I don't know if the rabbi survived the earthquake, but I'm sure his postings from the past few months are there."

"This is the man who was on television,"

Mr. Stein said. He rose and called for the guard. "I'll be back in the morning."

"You saved Chaya's Bible," Vicki said. "Why?"

Mr. Stein bowed his head. "Losing Chaya so soon after her mother's death was difficult. So I kept it. I can't tell you why."

"Have you read it?" Vicki said.

"I looked up the verse you talked about, but only for the purpose of helping you."

"You're a man of your word," Vicki said. "You promised Chaya you would find me, and you did. Now promise me something. No matter what happens to me, promise you'll look at that Web site and then read the Gospel of Matthew. It was written to Jewish people."

"I can't promise—"

"It would mean a lot to me," Vicki said.

The guard opened the cell door. Mr. Stein flipped to the first book of the New Testament and smiled. "I am a klutz when it comes to computers. But I will try to read this Matthew passage."

"I have your word?"

"You have my word."

Vicki smiled.

Judd tried to find out about Vicki through the Internet, but there was nothing. He e-mailed Tsion and asked the rabbi to pray. Judd suggested contacting Buck Williams, but Tsion said Buck wasn't available. He was still frantically looking for Chloe.

The kids talked about Ryan and traded stories. There were laughter and tears. Finally, Darrion said, "I think Shelly and I should go back to get Vicki."

"No way," Judd said.

Shelly said, "Darrion's right. It's dark. No one would see us. If they do, we'll say we're just looking for shelter."

"The GC have orders to shoot anyone moving around at night," Mark said. "We'd have to wait till morning."

"Vicki may not have that long," Darrion said.

"They'll probably send her to a reeducation camp like they did me," Judd said. "We can work on getting her out after she's sent there."

"Probably doesn't cut it," Darrion said. "That girl Joyce and the other two Morale Monitors have it in for her. If they believe she murdered her principal, they might give her the death penalty."

The four kids were silent. Judd thought of Vicki waiting in a cell. Or maybe they had already passed the sentence.

"We only have two options," Judd said. "We can try to find her and get her out, or we can wait and let Lionel and Conrad try. They're inside the GC machine."

"He's right," Mark said. "We have to trust Lionel and Conrad."

Lionel and Conrad secretly met outside the Global Community station.

"What happens if we get her out and then get caught?" Conrad said.

"We'd probably be shot for deserting," Lionel said.

Conrad sighed. "I don't see how we can let her go in there tomorrow morning. But I don't want the commander to pull the trigger on me either."

"He won't have the chance," Lionel said. "If my plan works, we'll be out of here by midnight. We can make it to the hideout before sunup."

"What if somebody sees us?"

"We're Morale Monitors," Lionel said. "We're searching for the other kid."

Conrad nodded. "All right, what's the plan?"

Judd and the others searched for blankets and pillows. Darrion said she was going upstairs to find a change of clothes. Mark surfed the Web for any information about Vicki. A few minutes later he called for Judd.

"Take a look at this on the Enigma Babylon page," Mark said.

Judd watched as an image of a smiling Pontifex Maximus Peter Mathews appeared on the screen. The man wore a huge hat and a funny outfit. Underneath was a message to "every soul on earth."

"Wherever you are in the world, whatever you're going through, know that Enigma Babylon One World Faith will be there. When disaster strikes, when governments fail, when your life crumbles before you, trust in Enigma Babylon."

"Looks like a commercial, doesn't it?" Mark said.

"The sad thing is, people will buy into it," Judd said.

Judd read on. "Don't be fooled by those who would cause you to fear for your future. Do not be led away from the hope of a new world order. Be part of a new breed of global citizenship."

"From reading that you'd think this Pontifex guy was competing with Carpathia," Mark said.

Judd sighed. "We've got bigger problems than Enigma Babylon right now."

Mark turned his chair toward Judd and spoke softly. "You're worried about her, aren't you?"

"I'm going out of my skin because there's nothing I can do. I want to march down there, grab Vicki, and run. But I know I can't."

Shelly burst into the room. "Have you guys seen Darrion?"

"I thought she went upstairs," Judd said.

"I've looked," Shelly said. "She's not upstairs or in the hangar."

Lionel found Melinda alone in a snack room at the station. He bought a drink and sat at a nearby table.

"Where's Felicia?" Lionel said.

Melinda didn't look up. "Went back to the shelter to get our stuff. We're staying here tonight."

"It'll be more comfortable than sleeping on the ground," Lionel said.

Melinda looked up. "What's with you? Why the small talk?"

"I'm really sorry about everything," Lionel said. "You guys were right. If I'd have listened to you, we'd have both of them in custody and the commander wouldn't be out a jeep."

"He told us he was going to have a talk with you tomorrow after the sentencing."

"I deserve it," Lionel said. "I just don't want this to break up the team."

Melinda eyed him warily. "You mean it?"

Lionel nodded. "Let me buy you some hot chocolate or something."

"Sure," Melinda said.

Lionel put money in the machine and turned his back to Melinda. "So why'd the commander rush out of here?"

"Didn't tell us," Melinda said, "but you know it has to be important. I think he wanted to finish with this girl tonight."

Lionel stirred the drink and handed it to her. "Know what I think? I say Vicki's in that cell thinking this is the last night of her life."

"It probably is."

"But what if it isn't?" Lionel said, dragging his chair close. "What if the commander buys into what that Stein guy says, that she's crazy or something."

"The commander's too smart for that—"

"Even in situations like this, you can't execute crazy people," Lionel said. "There's a chance he could send her to a reeducation site."

Melinda sipped her hot chocolate and shook her head. "He wouldn't do that. He can't. The girl murdered that principal."

"Melinda, there's a chance the commander might let her go. If he was going to give her a harsh sentence, why wouldn't he have done it before he ran out of here?"

Melinda took another sip.

"Now if I'm that girl," Lionel said, "and I'm thinking this is the last night of my life, I'd do or say anything to get out of it."

"What are you suggesting?"

"The commander wants the guy, Judd, right?"

"He'll find him."

"Eventually. But what if we get the information ourselves?"

"We don't have the commander's OK," Melinda said. "They won't even let us in to talk with her."

Conrad walked into the snack room. "What's up?"

Lionel filled him in.

"No way," Conrad said. "I'm in enough trouble with the commander as it is."

"This could get us all some points," Melinda said. "If we get the information, we can deliver this Judd guy by the time the commander passes sentence."

"Exactly," Lionel said.

Conrad crumpled his can of soda. "Call

me chicken or whatever you want, I'm not going down there."

Melinda drank the last of her hot chocolate. "I'm in. Let's go."

Judd led Shelly and Mark through the darkened house. Judd found the staircase that led upstairs. It was pitched at an angle and didn't look safe.

The three called for Darrion, but there was no answer.

"She told me her room was upstairs," Shelly said.

"Let me go first and see if it's safe," Judd said.

When he got to the middle, the staircase cracked and collapsed. Judd grabbed the railing overhead and pulled himself up. "You guys OK?" he said.

"Didn't hit us," Mark said. "See if you can find her room."

Judd knew where Mr. Stahley's office was. He went in and looked through the drawers. On the other side of the house he found Darrion's room. He tried a light, but the bulb was broken. The moonlight shone through the window. Judd saw clothes on the floor. He rushed to the stairs and used the railing to let himself down.

"She changed clothes upstairs," Judd said.

"The front door was open a bit," Mark said. "You think she's gone?"

"I think it's worse than that," Judd said. "Mr. Stahley's revolver is gone."

"You think Darrion has a gun?" Shelly said.

"Unless the looters got it."

An engine revved outside. Judd flew out the door in time to see a motorcycle bouncing through the grass near the entrance to the estate.

"Is that Darrion?" Shelly said.

"Has to be," Mark said, "but where'd she get the bike? Everything in the garage was gone."

"Stahley had all kinds of hiding places," Judd said. "Probably had the bike stashed for an emergency."

"Where do you think she's going?" Shelly said.

"She's trying to rescue Vick," Judd said.

Lionel knew he had to get Melinda into the cell quickly. Getting past the guard would be their major problem. But which tactic? Make the guard sympathize with them or play hardball?

"I don't have authorization to let you in," the guard said.

"The reason you don't have authorization

is Commander Blancka had to leave on important business," Lionel said. "He expects us to get the information from the girl tonight."

"Why do you think he delayed the sentencing?" Melinda said, scowling at the guard.

"I'd let you in if I had—"

"That's fine," Lionel said. "When the commander comes back here in the morning and finds out you wouldn't let us in, it's your problem, not ours."

Lionel pulled at Melinda's arm. "Let's get out of here."

"Wait," the guard said. "So, you just want to go talk with her, right?"

Melinda turned. "This guy who blew up the commander's jeep—she knows where he is. Now's our chance to get it from her."

"OK," the guard said. "I'll let you in. But you have to leave your weapons here and sign in."

Mitchell Stein opened his laptop. He took the scrap of paper and typed in the address. Reading the words of a traitor to his faith turned his stomach, but a promise was a promise.

Mr. Stein read through some of the E-mails

that had poured in since the earthquake. "These people are like sheep," he muttered.

He clicked on an icon that took him to a separate section written by Rabbi Ben-Judah.

> For those of you who still doubt our message, or who need the information to make an informed decision, I have written the following. The texts are found in the book of Romans, a logical layout of what we believe, written by the apostle Paul. Scholars have long been amazed at the sound reasoning and unity of thought contained in this book.

Mr. Stein wanted to stop, but something drew him to the words on the screen.

> Early in the book, Paul writes, "From the time the world was created, people have seen the earth and sky and all that God made. They can clearly see his invisible qualities—his eternal power and divine nature. So they have no excuse whatsoever for not knowing God."
>
> If it is true that God has put the knowledge of himself on our hearts, what would keep a person from under-

> standing the true and living God? The answer is found two chapters away. "For all have sinned; all fall short of God's glorious standard." A little further in the book Paul writes, "For the wages of sin is death, but the free gift of God is eternal life through Christ Jesus our Lord."

Mr. Stein read on about God's Law and how people had tried to make a way to God themselves. The rabbi wrote:

> It will not work. God's Law is holy and perfect and can accept nothing but perfection. You and I are imperfect. The more you read about God's Law, the more you understand how imperfect we are.

That is true, Mr. Stein thought.

> The only way to God is through accepting the gift he has given in Jesus. He lived a perfect life. He died in our place. He took the penalty for our sin. "Salvation that comes from trusting Christ . . . is already within easy reach," Paul wrote. "For if you confess with your mouth that Jesus is Lord and believe in your heart that God raised him from the

> dead, you will be saved. For it is by believing in your heart that you are made right with God, and it is by confessing with your mouth that you are saved."

There were more verses and a prayer the rabbi included at the end, but Mr. Stein couldn't read any further. He sat back in his chair and stared at the ceiling. He had believed his wife and daughter were mistaken. He had thought they were confused about their faith. Now he was confused.

TEN

Springing Vicki

VICKI was glad to see Lionel, then she noticed Melinda behind him. Lionel unlocked the cell door, and the two walked in. Vicki sat up on her cot and looked them over. Lionel and Melinda stared at her.

"What's up?" Vicki said. "Has the commander decided?"

"What do *you* think?" Melinda said. "You counting on him letting you out of here?"

"I don't know what he'll do," Vicki said. "All I know is that I'm innocent."

Lionel laughed. "That's a good one. You're as innocent as those militia people."

Vicki couldn't believe Lionel would turn on her like this. Had he lost his memory again?

"You've only got one hope now, Byrne," Melinda said. "You tell us what you know about this Judd Thompson, and we'll have a talk with the commander before he sentences you."

"I don't know where—"

"Think hard before you answer," Lionel said, getting down in Vicki's face. Lionel winked. "Tell us where you and Judd were going before we caught you."

Vicki felt relieved. Lionel was up to something. She wanted to play along but didn't know what to say. Finally, she said, "If I tell you, what happens to Judd?"

"What is he, your boyfriend?" Melinda said. "Do yourself a favor and give him up."

"All right," Vicki said. "If you promise to talk to the commander."

Judd and the others looked in the garage, but there were no vehicles left. The Stahleys' cars had either been stolen or taken by the GC.

"What do you think she'll do?" Mark said.

"Who knows," Judd said. "She's lost her mother and father, and now Ryan's dead. She'll probably risk it and go into the GC camp and wave that gun around."

"She doesn't even know where they're holding Vicki, if she's still alive," Shelly said.

"Vick's alive," Judd said. "She has to be."

Lionel shouted at Vicki. He glanced away and saw Melinda put her hand to her head and wince. Just a few more minutes and his plan would work.

"Judd and I were headed back to the church," Vicki said. "There's an underground hideout there. And we would have made it if that stupid chopper hadn't shown up."

"You were miles from the church when they found you," Melinda said.

"We tried to throw the GC off by driving away," Vicki said.

Melinda sat on the floor. "I don't feel so good." She rubbed her head and moaned.

Lionel knelt beside her. "What's the matter?"

"It's my head," she said, running a hand through her hair. "Everything's spinning. I want to go back to the other room."

"Should I call for the guard?" Vicki said.

"No," Lionel snapped. "Just lie down. You'll be OK in a minute."

Melinda's eyes widened. "You! You put something in my drink!" She reached for a cell bar to pull herself up, but Lionel grabbed her and put a hand over her mouth. Melinda tried to shout, but she was helpless.

"Help me get her to the bed," Lionel said to Vicki.

Vicki grabbed Melinda's arm, and the two dragged the girl to Vicki's cot. By the time her head hit the pillow, Melinda had passed out.

"Listen close," Lionel said. "We're not out of this yet. I'm going down the hall to signal Conrad. You change clothes with Melinda. When Conrad comes, you have to be ready."

"What about the guard?" Vicki said. "He'll know!"

"That's where Conrad comes in," Lionel said. "You have three minutes to make the change."

With tears streaming down her face, Darrion flew into the night. She hated going against Judd and the others, but she couldn't sit still and watch another person she loved die without a fight. Vicki had taken her in and helped her when it seemed the whole world was against her. Darrion couldn't bear the thought of Vicki's execution or even imprisonment.

She felt the gun on her hip and wondered if she would have to use it. She wished she had tried to rescue her mother before the earthquake. She wouldn't make the same mistake again. Still, Darrion had no idea how she would find Vicki or get her out. But she knew she had to try.

Darrion had believed in Christ long enough to know she needed God's help to do anything. But she couldn't think of that now. She didn't even want to pray. God didn't seem to be doing anything to help her friends, so she would take over.

Darrion's father had taught her a lot about motorcycles. But nothing had prepared her for this ride. The road was jagged, and she nearly lost control several times. She slowed when the beam of her headlight shone on water.

I have to cross the river.

She backtracked along the bank until she saw work crews with huge lights working on a bridge. The top of the bridge was intact, but the pavement had crumbled. The GC workers pounded nails in boards.

The workers looked up as Darrion gunned the engine and shot past them across the rickety boards.

"She'll never make it to the end," someone shouted.

But Darrion had been trained well. She picked her way through the shaky maze of boards and steel girders. The lights showed a huge gap between the end of the bridge and the riverbank. She gunned the engine again, shot past the last row of men, and soared into the air.

Lionel ran to the back of the jail and signaled Conrad with his flashlight. A moment later Conrad sent an identical message back.

"Good," Lionel said. "Everything's working."

Lionel quickly moved to the front door and listened for the guard. A cell phone rang. The guard said, "Hello? Hello?"

Lionel ran back to Vicki. Melinda lay limp on the cot in Vicki's dirty clothes.

"What did you give her?" Vicki said. "She's totally out."

"I saved a couple of sleeping pills they gave me after the earthquake," Lionel said. "One pill helped me sleep. I figured two would knock her out."

"What happens—?" Vicki said.

"I don't have time to explain. When I give the word, you hustle past Conrad and me and head for the front door. Don't stop for anybody, got it?"

"Got it," Vicki said. "But—"

Lionel held up a hand. A door opened outside. Conrad shouted something.

"She's in there," the guard said.

On cue, Conrad burst into the cell area and shouted, "Where's Melinda? Commander Blancka wants her right away!"

"Commander Blancka!" Lionel shouted. "Come on, let's get you out of here."

Vicki ran past Lionel. Conrad blocked the view of the guard.

"Hey, you have to sign out," the guard shouted as Vicki ran out the door.

"I'll sign for her," Lionel said.

"I wonder what the commander wants," Conrad said.

"Must be pretty important," Lionel said as he signed his name and Melinda's.

"Did you get that girl to talk?" the guard said.

"She clammed up," Lionel said. "Went to sleep. We gotta get outta here and see what the commander wants. Thanks for your help."

Lionel and Conrad followed Vicki a few blocks away. They ducked into a darkened alley. All three were out of breath.

"I'm staying," Conrad said.

"No way," Lionel said. "We agreed as soon as Vicki was free, you'd get out of here."

"We need somebody inside," Conrad said.

"They'll pin this on you," Lionel said.

"I'll tell them I got a call from someone who said they were an aide to Commander Blancka. What was I supposed to do—ignore it?"

Lionel bit his lip. The plan made sense, but he knew Conrad was scared of staying with the GC. "Are you sure?"

Conrad nodded. The three put their hands together.

"God go with you," Conrad said.

"You too," Vicki said. She hugged him.

"Let's go," Lionel said.

Vicki's ankle felt much better. She and Lionel ran side by side. Vicki got her bearings and noticed some of the same neighborhoods she and Judd had gone through.

"Someday you're going to have to tell me how you got mixed up with these morale people," Vicki whispered.

"Just get me to the Stahley place and I'll tell you anything you want to know," Lionel said.

As they came over a hill, a light hit them from below. Vicki ducked, then started back. Lionel grabbed her arm.

"Stop or we'll shoot!" a man shouted from below.

Lionel whispered to Vicki, "You're a Morale Monitor, remember that." He put his hands over his head and led Vicki down the hill. When they came close to the GC guards, Lionel said, "We're working with Commander Blancka on finding a missing kid."

"Where's your side arm?" the guard said suspiciously.

Lionel winced. "It's a long story. Commander Blancka said we had to find this guy or we'd get the same punishment. We let him get away."

"Him?" the guard said. "Too bad. I thought I might be able to help you."

"What do you mean?" Lionel said.

"We picked up a girl on a motorcycle about ten minutes ago," the guard said. "She had a GC-registered side arm. Wouldn't give us her name."

"Doesn't sound like who we're looking for," Lionel said. "We're looking for a Judd Thompson."

"I'll send a report to the other patrols," the guard said. "Give me your names."

Lionel gave him his name and Melinda's. When the guard was gone he said, "That was close."

"What happened to your gun?" Vicki said.

"Left it when we got you out," Lionel said.

"It's a good thing we didn't run away from them," Vicki said. "I just don't want to be out here when they find Sleeping Beauty in that cell."

Judd didn't sleep all night. He paced the floor of the computer room, then moved upstairs when he saw he was keeping the others awake. His body wasn't on the same schedule as everyone else's.

It was nearly sunup when he finally sat on the couch and grew tired. A noise startled him. He heard footsteps in the kitchen, and voices.

GC, Judd thought. *They've caught Darrion, and she led them back here.* Judd scooted down on the couch and reached for his gun. These guys wouldn't take him without a fight.

The voices came nearer. "It's gotta be around here somewhere," one said.

"I thought they said it was near a hallway that led to the kitchen," another said.

Judd peeked over the top of the couch. He clicked the safety off and yelled, "Hold it right there!"

The two scrambled backward and put up their hands. "Don't shoot!" one of them said.

Judd stood and walked closer.

"Judd, is that you?" a girl said.

"Vicki?" Judd said.

Judd finally saw their faces. *Vicki and Lionel.* A wave of relief swept over him. He put the gun away. Vicki ran to him and they embraced. Judd put an arm around Lionel.

"I didn't know if I'd ever see you guys again," Judd said.

"It wasn't easy," Lionel said. He told Judd the story of their escape and meeting the GC patrol. "We had to talk our way across a bridge. I'm glad we're finally safe. All except Conrad."

"And Darrion," Judd said. "She took off last night on her dad's motorcycle."

Vicki gasped. "The patrol said they'd taken a girl on a motorcycle into custody."

Judd sat down hard on the sofa. "Once the GC figure out who she is, she's in big trouble."

"We're all in trouble," Vicki said.

"You think she'd lead them back here?" Lionel said.

"Not on purpose," Vicki said, "but they'd be able to trace that bike."

Conrad and Felicia were waiting at the door the next morning when Commander Blancka walked in. "Why did you want to see Melinda last night, sir?"

"What are you talking about?" the commander said.

"I got a call last night that said you wanted to see Melinda. The man said it was urgent and she should meet you at the helipad."

"I never gave that order," the commander said. He looked at Felicia. "Go check on her."

"I was there all night, sir," Felicia said. "Melinda never returned."

The commander glared at Conrad.

"I went down to the cell to give her the message—"

"What cell?" the commander said.

"Where you were keeping that girl, Vicki. That's where Lionel and Melinda were."

The commander barked into his radio as Conrad continued. "I saw them in the snack room. They were planning on getting information out of that girl. They wanted to find the guy by this morning and impress you."

The guard at the cell block said Melinda and Lionel had signed out late the previous night.

"Bring the Byrne girl here immediately," the commander said.

Mr. Stein came in. Conrad thought he looked upset.

"Have you reached a decision, sir?" Mr. Stein said.

"You'll find out soon enough," the commander said.

"Sir, if you intend to execute this young lady, I must know now."

The commander stiffened. "Sit down and wait."

The guard hustled into the room. Behind him was the groggy prisoner. "She's out of her head. Says she was tricked."

Felicia gasped. "Melinda!"

The commander slammed his fist on the table. He looked at Mr. Stein. "You tricked my guard!"

"I did nothing of the sort," Mr. Stein said.

The commander fumed. "You're all under arrest until I find the person responsible for this!"

About the Authors

Jerry B. Jenkins (www.jerryjenkins.com) is the writer of the Left Behind series. He is author of more than one hundred books, of which ten have reached the *New York Times* best-seller list. Former vice president for publishing for the Moody Bible Institute of Chicago, he also served many years as editor of *Moody* magazine and is now Moody's writer-at-large.

His writing has appeared in publications as varied as *Reader's Digest, Parade,* in-flight magazines, and many Christian periodicals. He has written books in four genres: biography, marriage and family, fiction for children, and fiction for adults.

Jenkins's biographies include books with Hank Aaron, Bill Gaither, Luis Palau, Walter Payton, Orel Hershiser, Nolan Ryan, Brett Butler, and Billy Graham, among many others.

Seven of his apocalyptic novels—*Left Behind, Tribulation Force, Nicolae, Soul Harvest, Apollyon, Assassins,* and *The Indwelling*—have appeared on the Christian Booksellers Association's best-selling fiction list and the *Publishers Weekly* religion best-seller list. *Left Behind* was nominated for Book of the Year by the Evangelical Christian Publishers Association in 1997, 1998, 1999, and 2000. *The Indwelling* was number one on the *New York Times* best-seller list for four consecutive weeks.

As a marriage and family author and speaker, Jenkins has been a frequent guest on Dr. James Dobson's *Focus on the Family* radio program.

Jerry is also the writer of the nationally syndicated sports story comic strip *Gil Thorp,* distributed to newspapers across the United States by Tribune Media Services.

Jerry and his wife, Dianna, live in Colorado.

Dr. Tim LaHaye (www.timlahaye.com), who conceived the idea of fictionalizing an account of the Rapture and the Tribulation, is a noted author, minister, and nationally recognized speaker on Bible prophecy. He is the founder of both Tim LaHaye Ministries and The Pre-Trib Research Center. Presently Dr. LaHaye speaks at many of the major Bible prophecy conferences in the U.S. and Canada, where his nine current prophecy books are very popular.

Dr. LaHaye holds a doctor of ministry degree from Western Theological Seminary and the doctor of literature degree from Liberty University. For twenty-five years he pastored one of the nation's outstanding churches in San Diego, which grew to three locations. It was during that time that he founded two accredited Christian high schools, a Christian school system of ten schools, and Christian Heritage College.

Dr. LaHaye has written over forty books, with over 30 million copies in print in thirty-three languages. He has written books on a wide variety of subjects, such as family life, temperaments, and Bible prophecy. His current fiction works, written with Jerry Jenkins—*Left Behind, Tribulation Force, Nicolae, Soul Harvest, Apollyon, Assassins,* and *The Indwelling*—have all reached number one on the Christian best-seller charts. Other works by Dr. LaHaye are *Spirit-Controlled Temperament; How to Be Happy Though Married; Revelation Unveiled; Understanding the Last Days; Rapture under Attack; Are We Living in the End Times?;* and the youth fiction series Left Behind: The Kids.

He is the father of four grown children and grandfather of nine. Snow skiing, waterskiing, motorcycling, golfing, vacationing with family, and jogging are among his leisure activities.

#11: Into the Storm The search for secret documents.

#12: Earthquake! The Young Trib Force faces disaster.

#13: The Showdown Behind enemy lines.

#14: Judgment Day Into raging waters.

BOOKS #15 AND #16 COMING SOON!